NUGGET AND DOG

YUM FEST IS THE BEST!

YF
YF

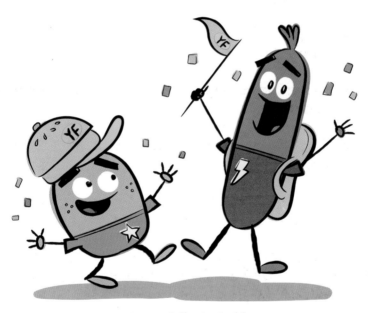

written and illustrated by
JASON THARP

Ready-to-Read *GRAPHICS*

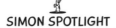

SIMON SPOTLIGHT
An imprint of Simon & Schuster Children's Publishing Division • New York • London • Toronto • Sydney • New Delhi
1230 Avenue of the Americas, New York, New York 10020 • This Simon Spotlight edition August 2021
 For information about special discounts for bulk purchases, please contact Simon & Schuster Special Sales at 1-866-506-1949 or business@simonandschuster.com. Manufactured in the United States of America 0721 LAK
1 2 3 4 5 6 7 8 9 10 • This book has been cataloged with the Library of Congress.
ISBN 978-1-5344-8466-5 (hc) • ISBN 978-1-5344-8465-8 (pbk) • ISBN 978-1-5344-8467-2 (ebook)

To the readers,
Love is a powerful thing especially when you use it to love yourself.
Special thanks to the S&S crew who put a lot of love into this book:
Beth, Laura, Nicole, and Siobhan.
—J. T.

You can be a K.E.T.C.H.U.P. Crusader anytime, remember it's:

Kind
Empathetic
Thoughtful
Courageous
Helpful
Unique
Powerful

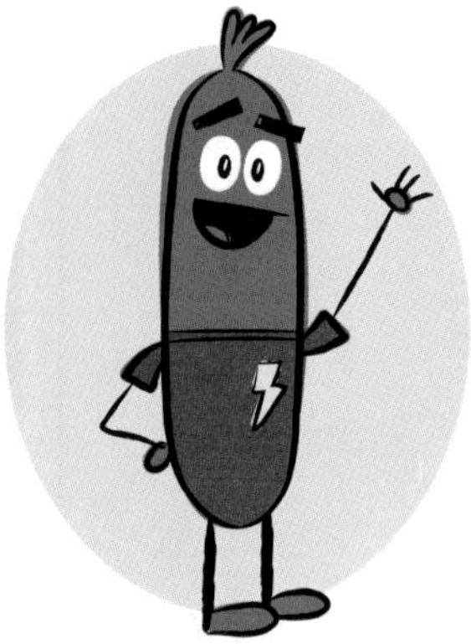

Dog

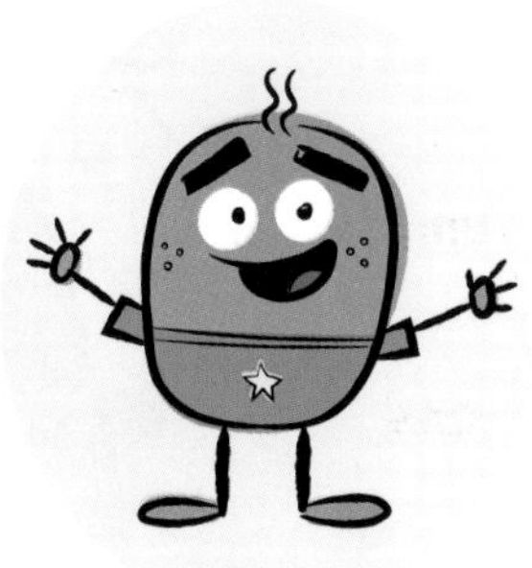

Nugget

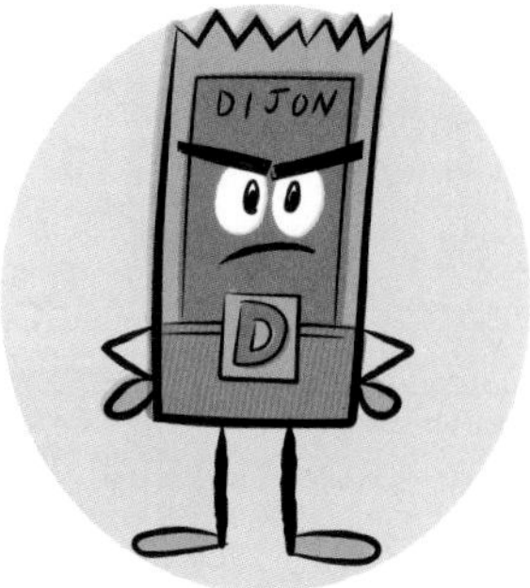
DIJON
D

Dijon (say: dee-ZHON)
Mustard

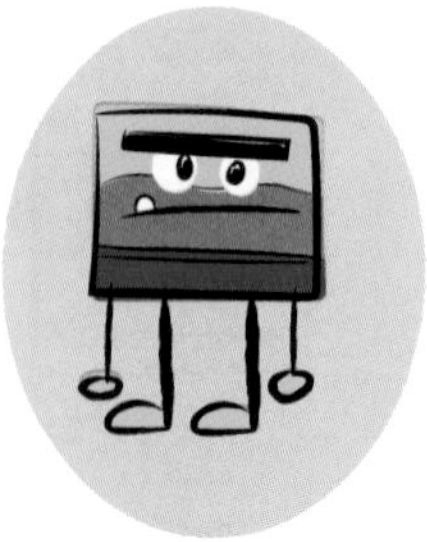

Crouton
(say: KROO-tahn)

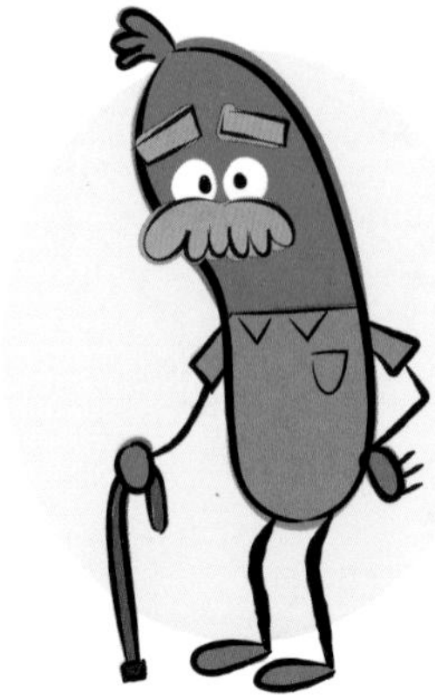

Great-Grandpa
Frank Furter

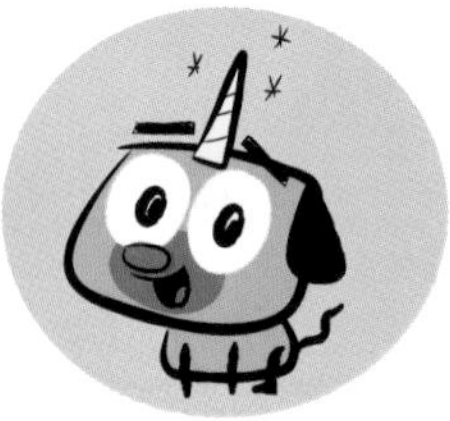

Buttercup

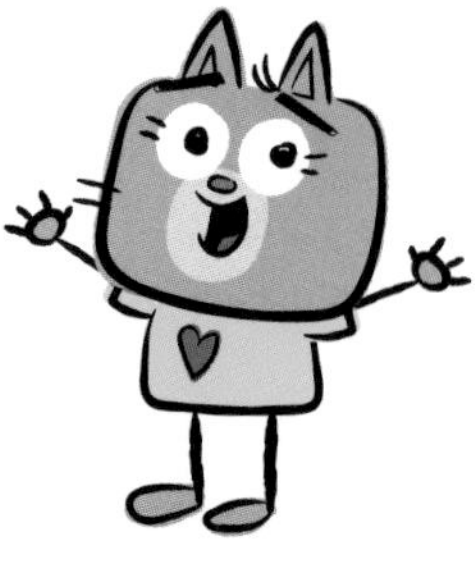

Ginger Jam

CONTENTS

How to Read This Book

This is Dog. He is here to give you some tips on how to read this book.

If there is a box like this one, read the words inside the box first. Then read the words in the speech or thought bubbles below it...

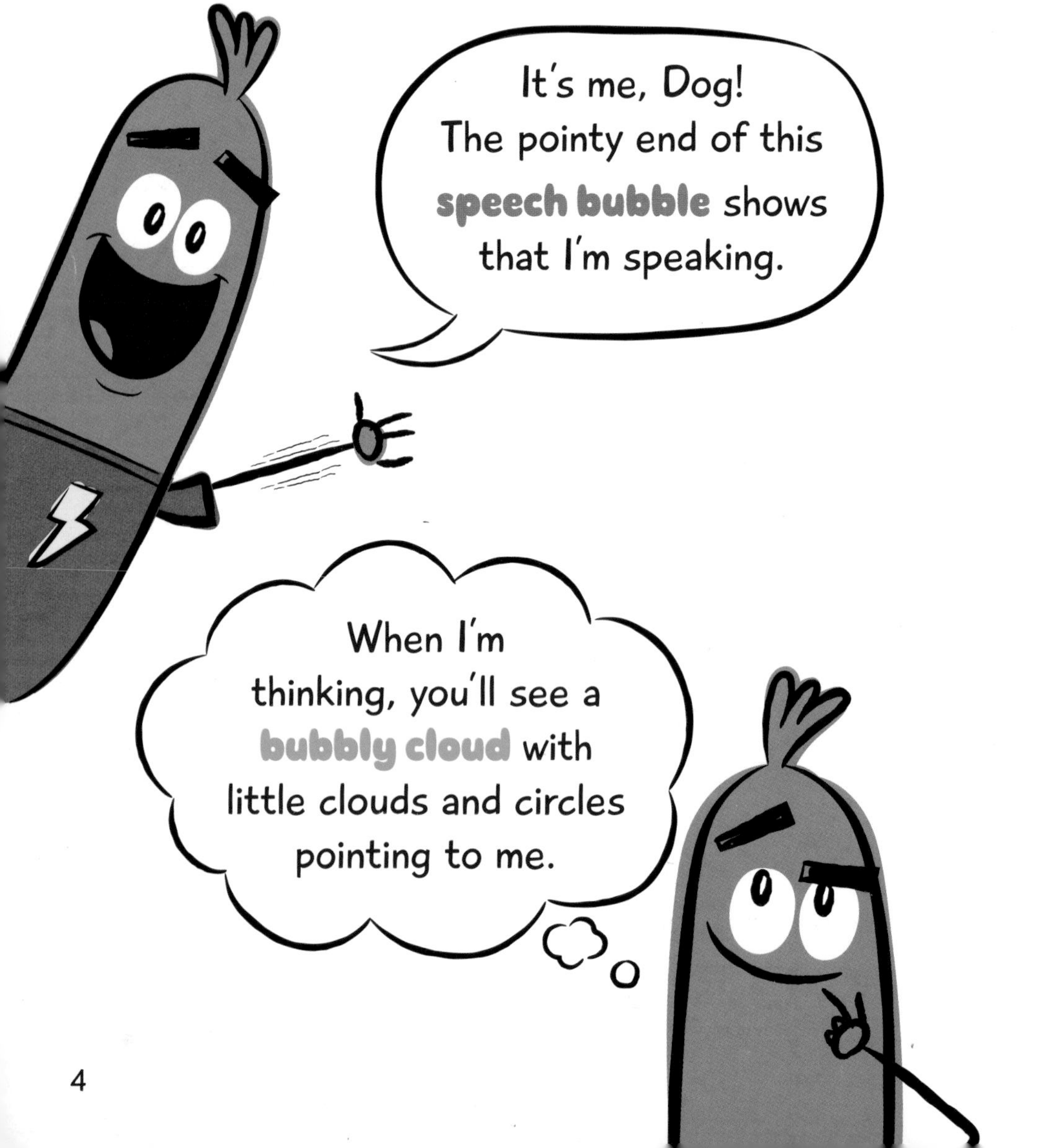
It's me, Dog! The pointy end of this speech bubble shows that I'm speaking.
When I'm thinking, you'll see a bubbly cloud with little clouds and circles pointing to me.

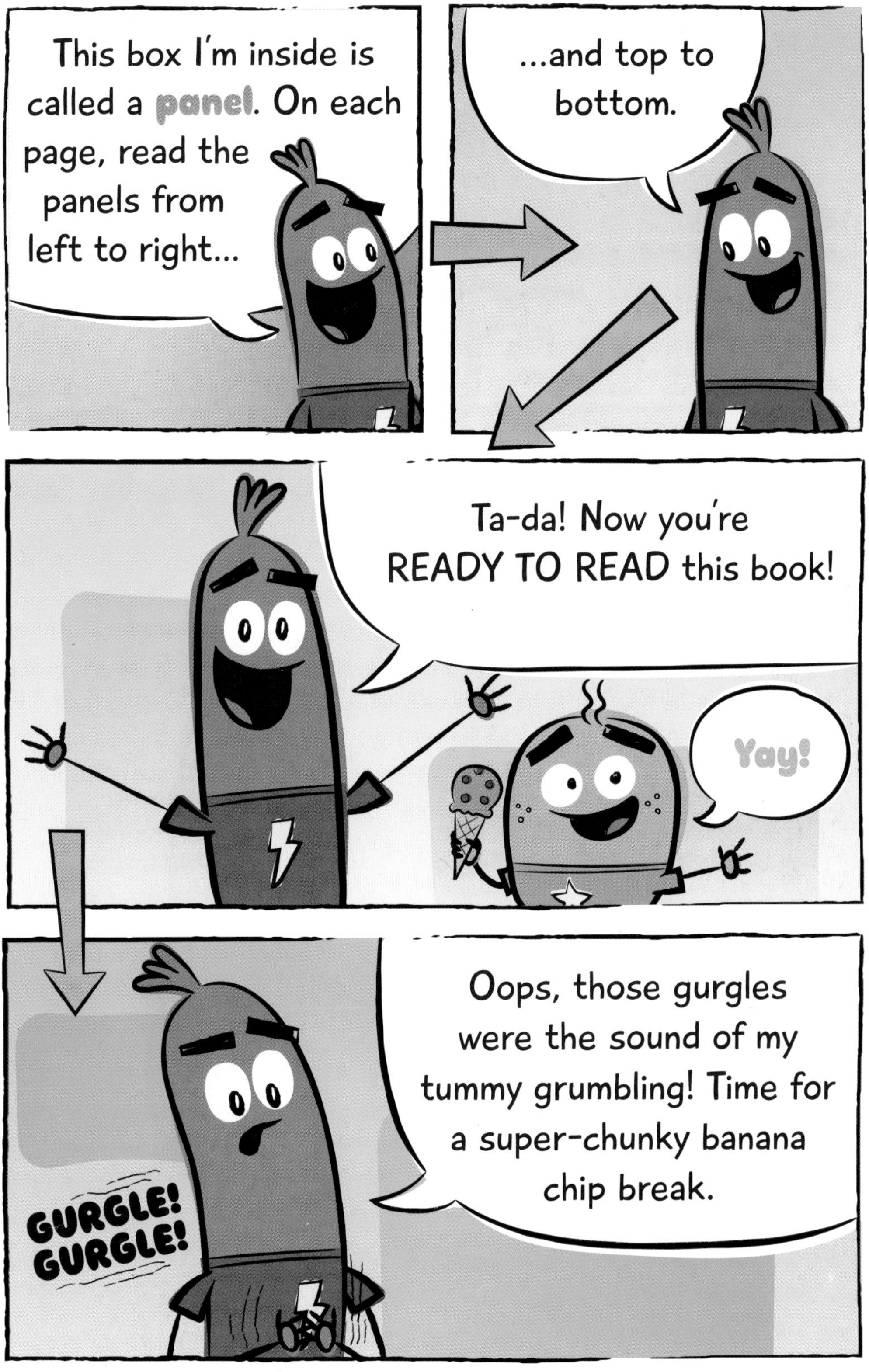
This box I'm inside is called a panel. On each page, read the panels from left to right...
...and top to bottom.
Ta-da! Now you're READY TO READ this book!
Yay!
Oops, those gurgles were the sound of my tummy grumbling! Time for a super-chunky banana chip break.
GURGLE! GURGLE!

Chapter 1

LET'S K.E.T.C.H.U.P.!

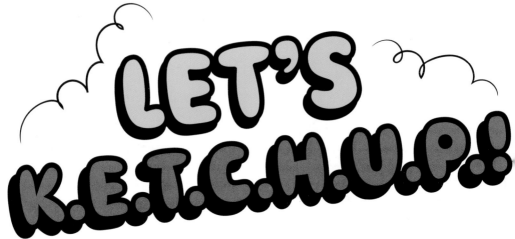

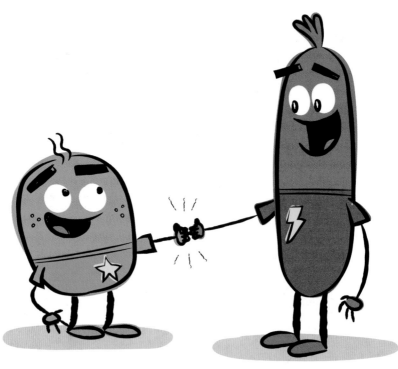

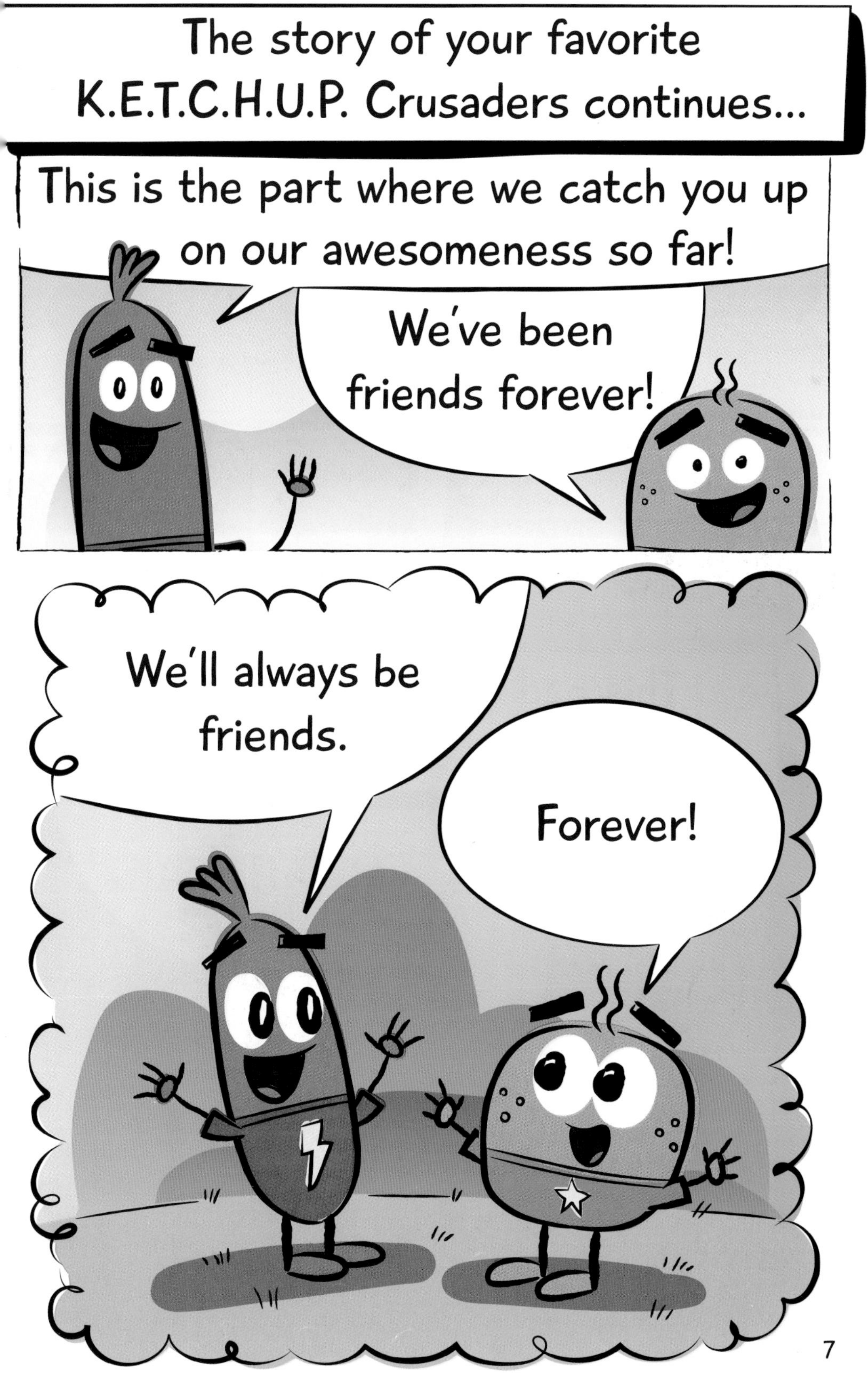
The story of your favorite
K.E.T.C.H.U.P. Crusaders continues...
This is the part where we catch you up on our awesomeness so far!
We've been friends forever!
We'll always be friends.
Forever!

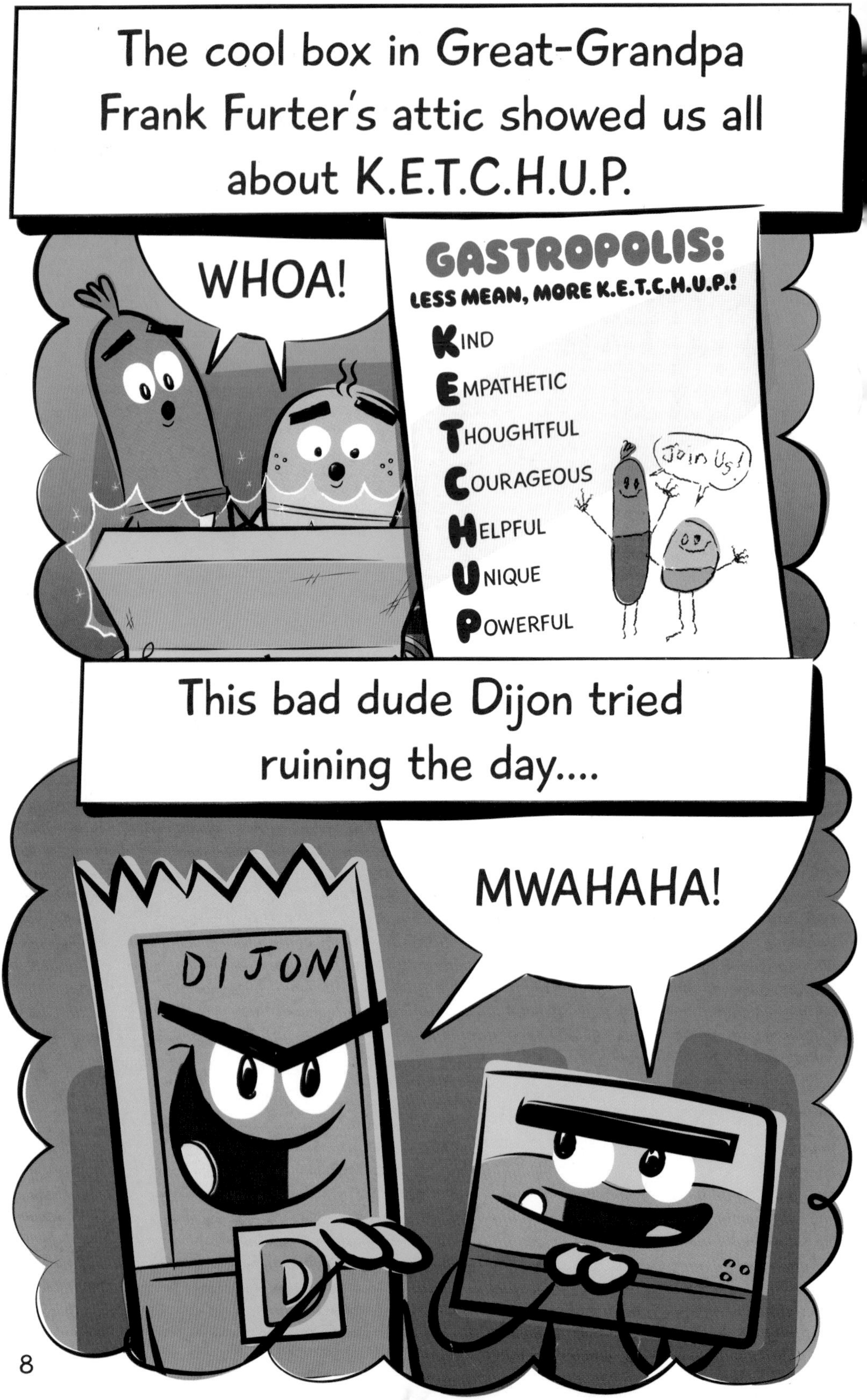
The cool box in Great-Grandpa Frank Furter's attic showed us all about K.E.T.C.H.U.P.
WHOA!
GASTROPOLIS:
LESS MEAN, MORE K.E.T.C.H.U.P.!
KIND
EMPATHETIC
THOUGHTFUL
COURAGEOUS
HELPFUL
UNIQUE
POWERFUL
Join Us!
This bad dude Dijon tried ruining the day....
DIJON
MWAHAHA!
D

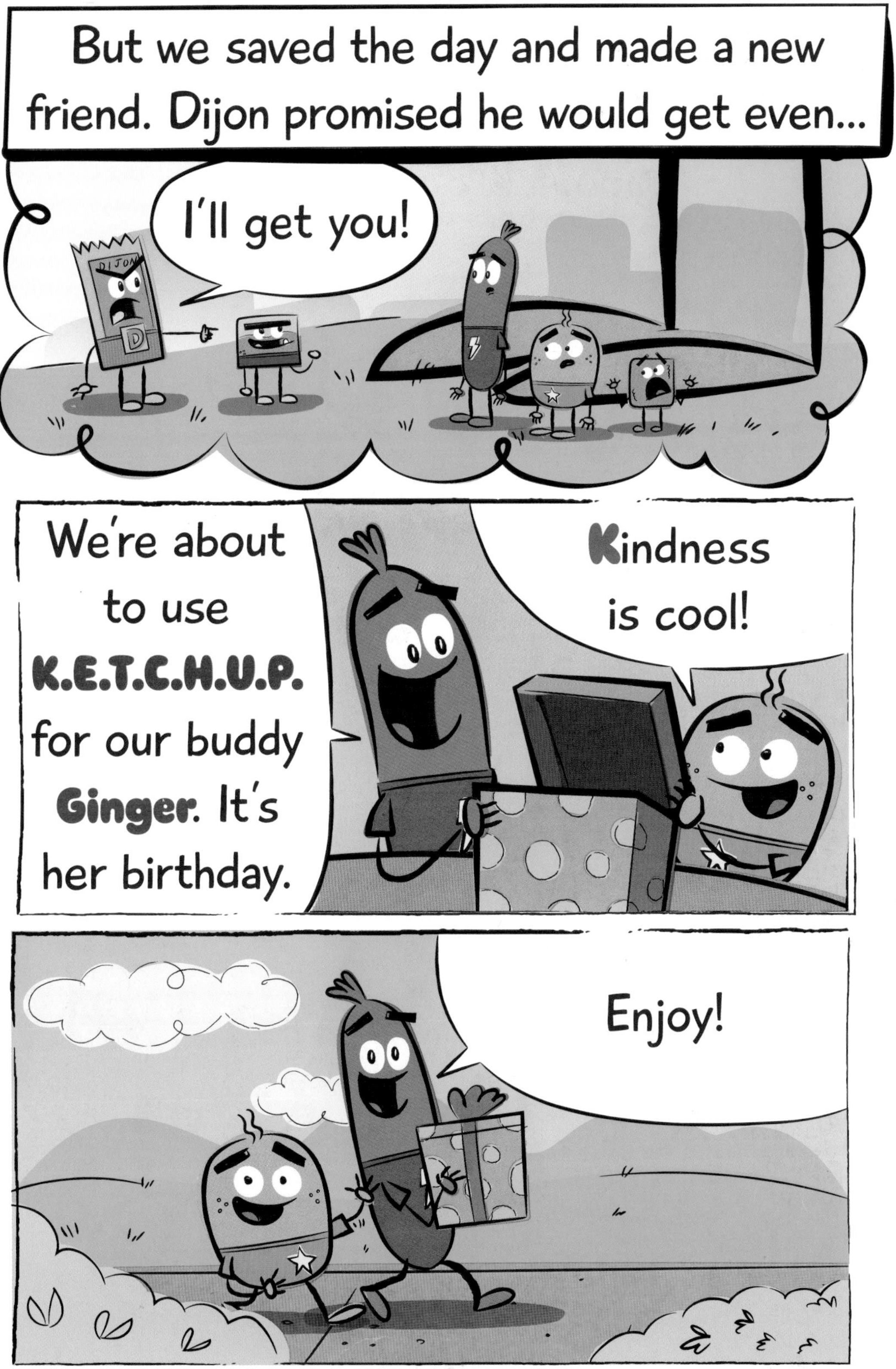
But we saved the day and made a new friend. Dijon promised he would get even...
I'll get you!
DIJON
We're about to use K.E.T.C.H.U.P. for our buddy Ginger. It's her birthday.
Kindness is cool!
Enjoy!

Chapter 2

PARTY TIME!

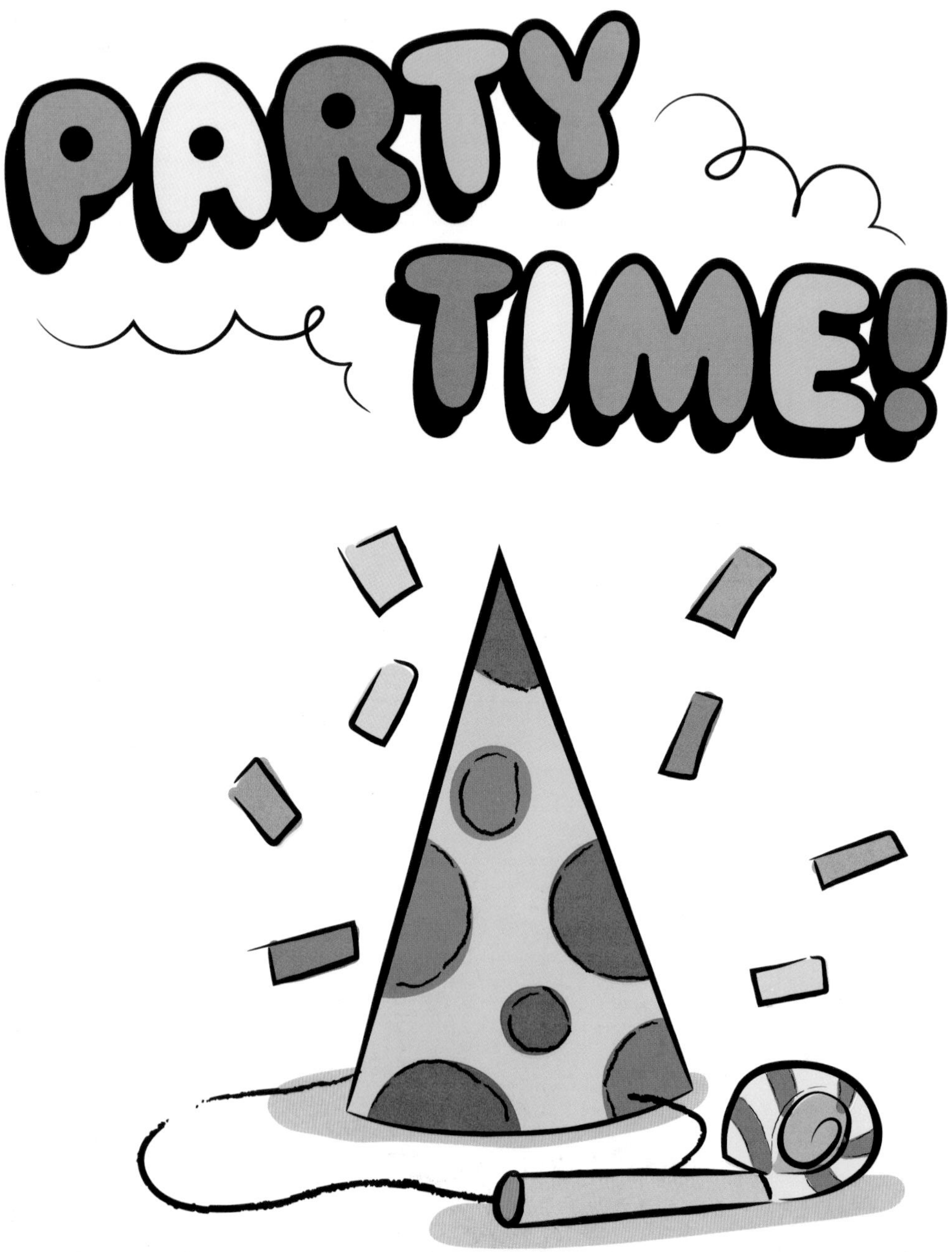

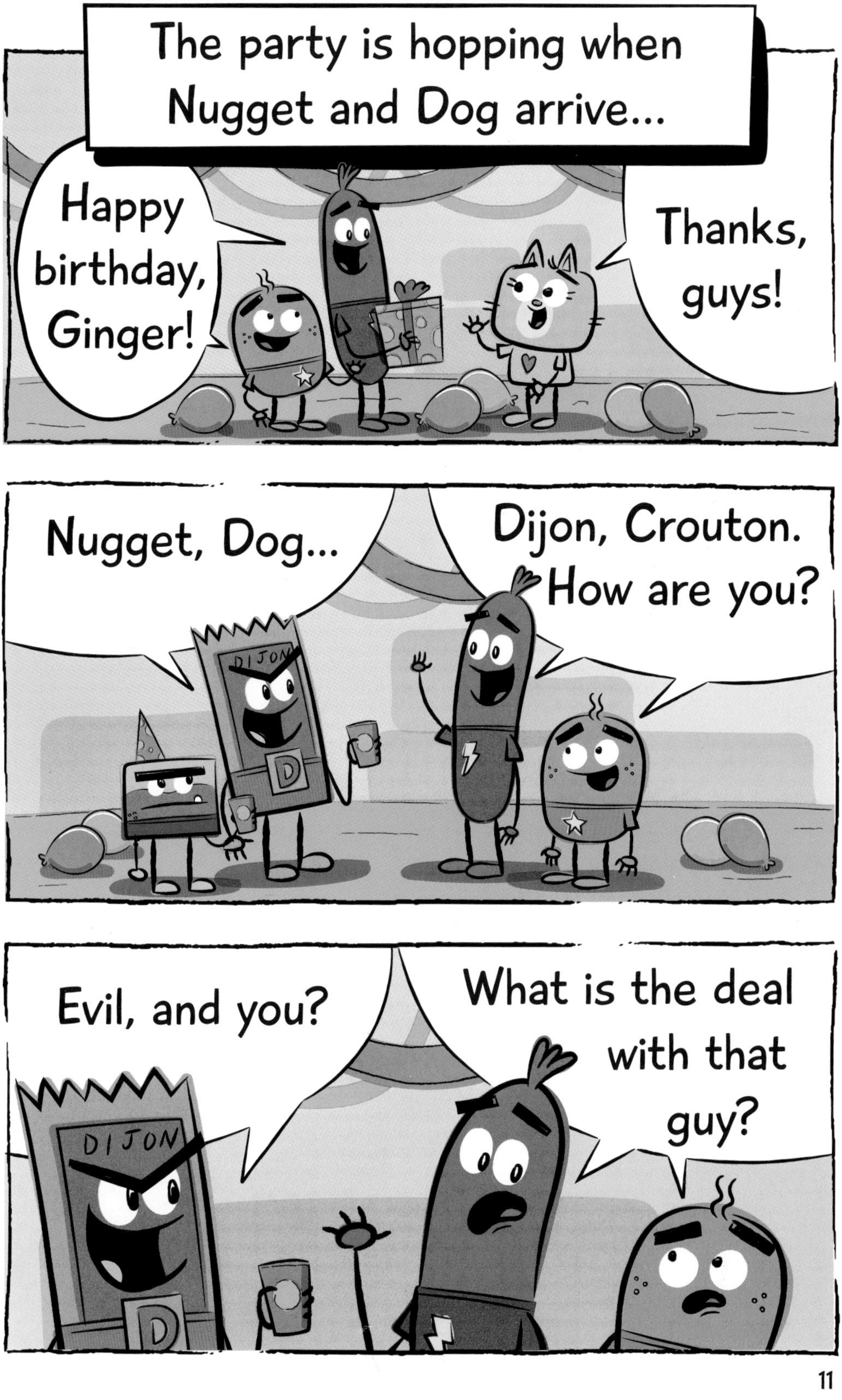
The party is hopping when Nugget and Dog arrive...
Happy birthday, Ginger!
Thanks, guys!
Nugget, Dog...
Dijon, Crouton. How are you?
DIJON
D
Evil, and you?
What is the deal with that guy?
DIJON
D

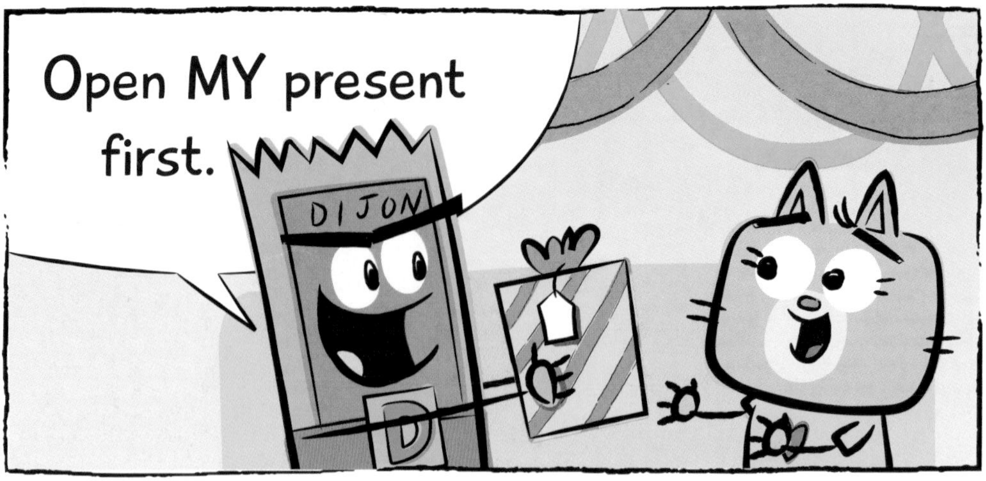
Open MY present first.
DIJON
D

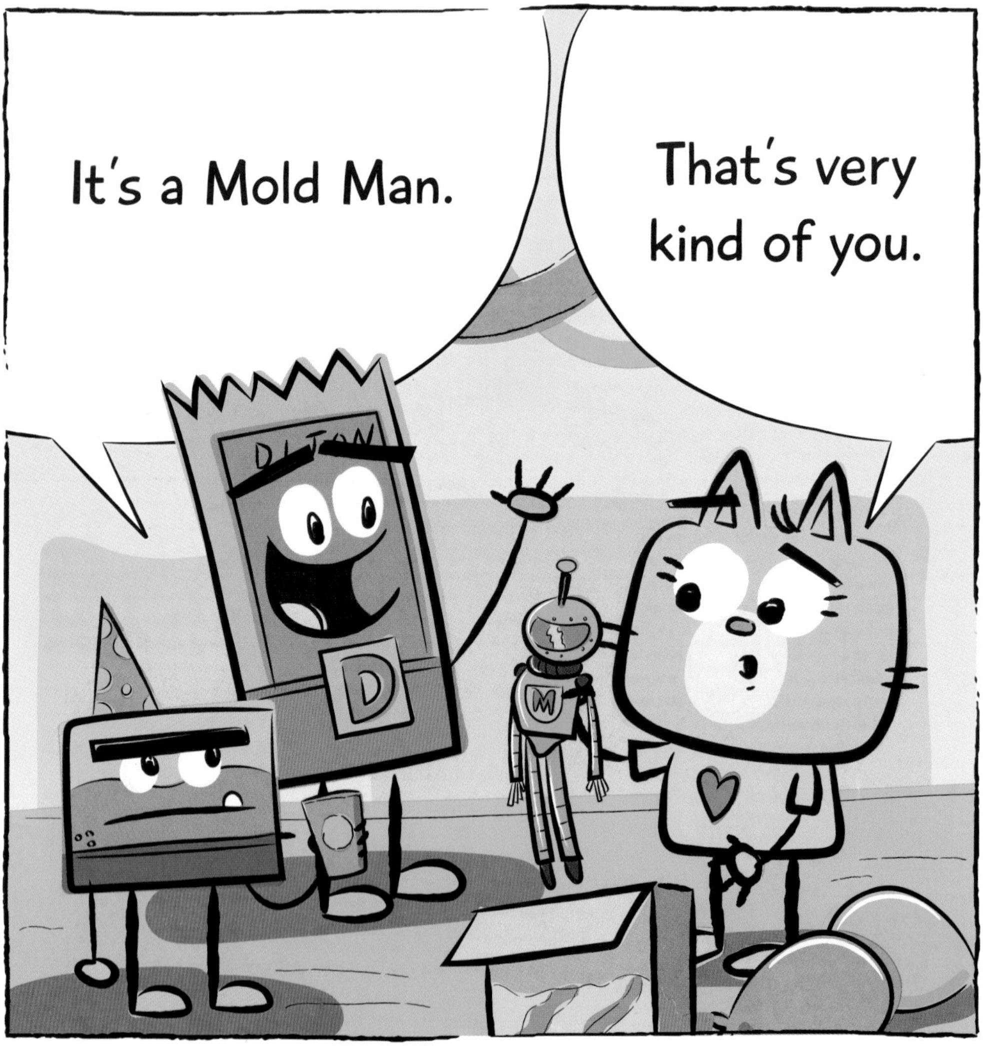
It's a Mold Man.
That's very kind of you.
D
M

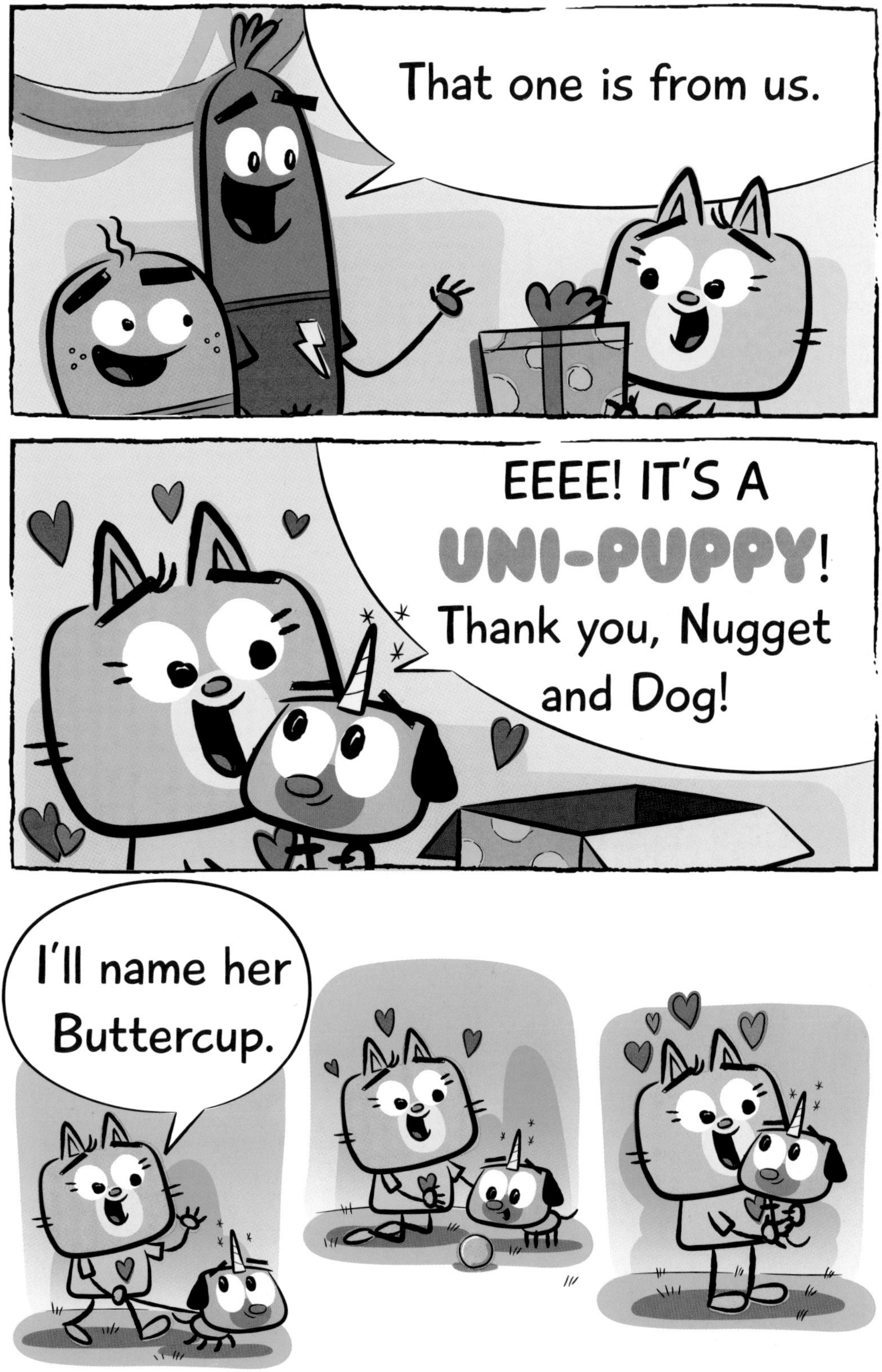
That one is from us.
EEEE! IT'S A UNI-PUPPY! Thank you, Nugget and Dog!
I'll name her Buttercup.

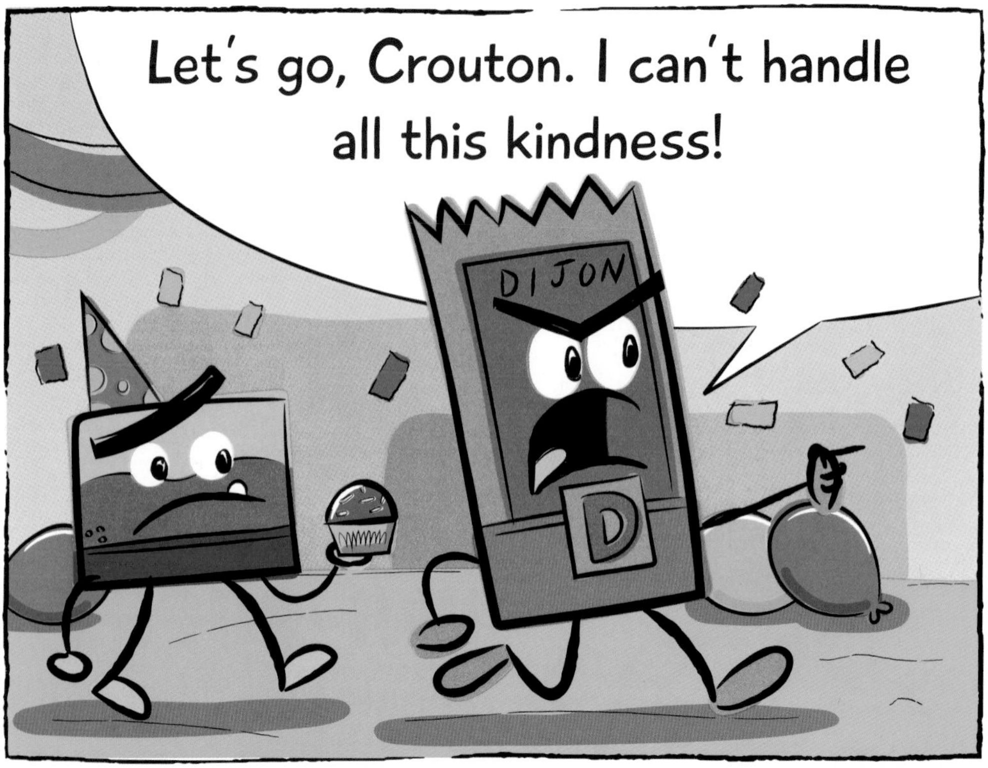
Let's go, Crouton. I can't handle all this kindness!
DIJON
D

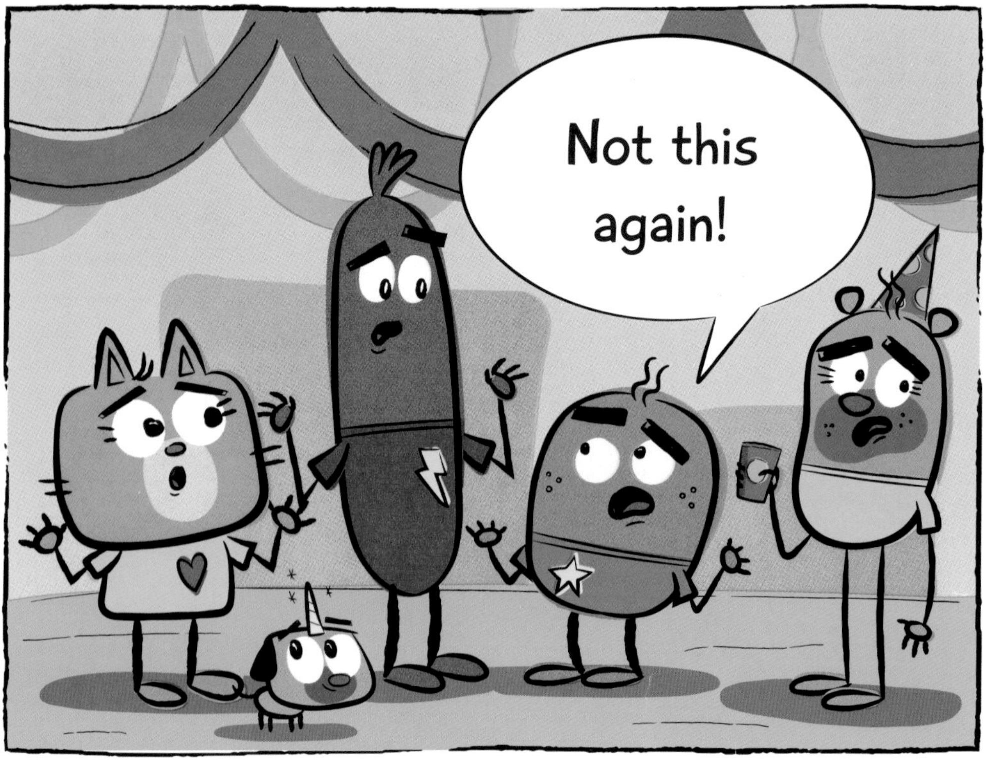
Not this again!

Chapter 3

LET THE YUM BEGIN!

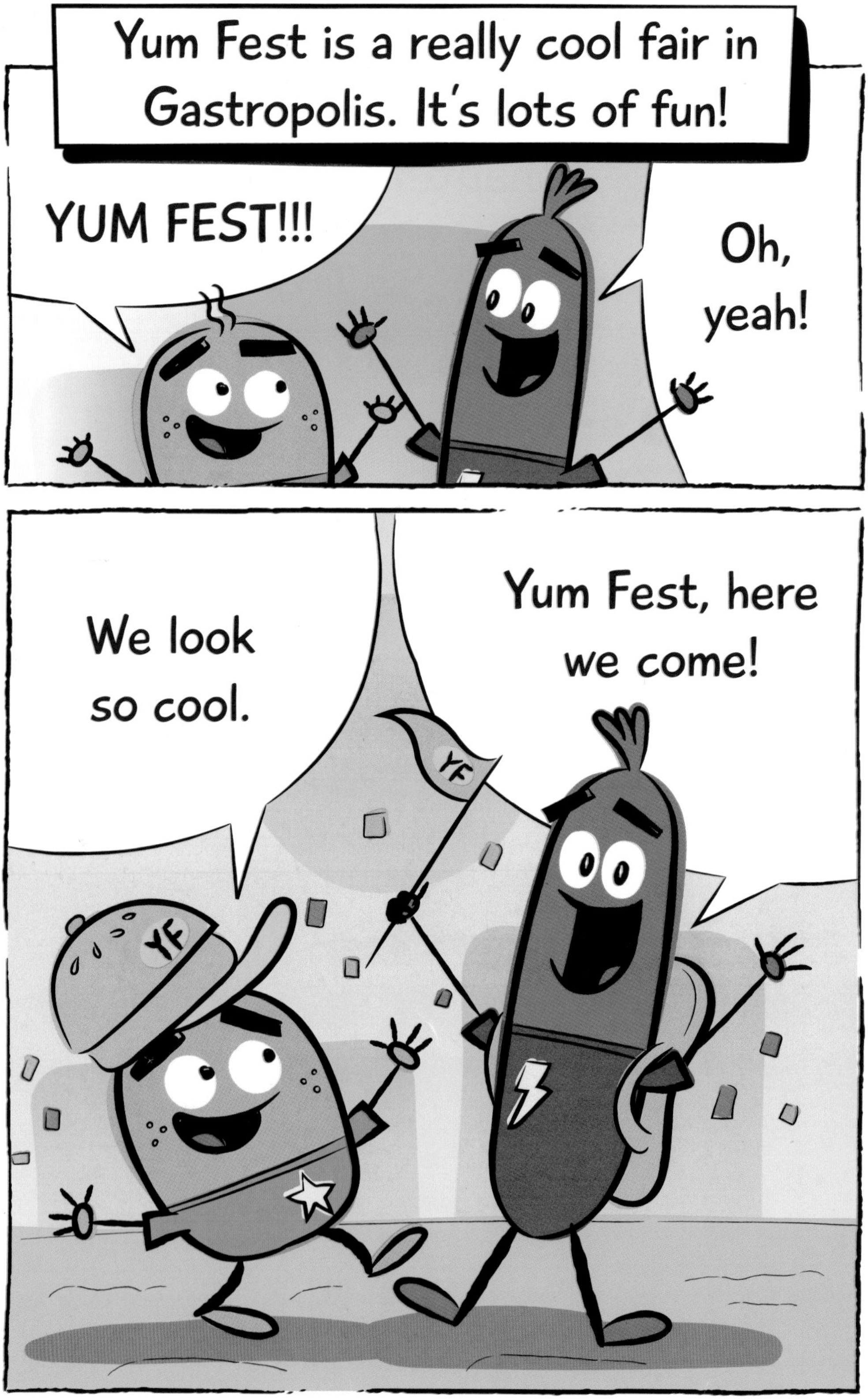
Yum Fest is a really cool fair in Gastropolis. It's lots of fun!
YUM FEST!!!
Oh, yeah!
We look so cool.
Yum Fest, here we come!
YF
YF

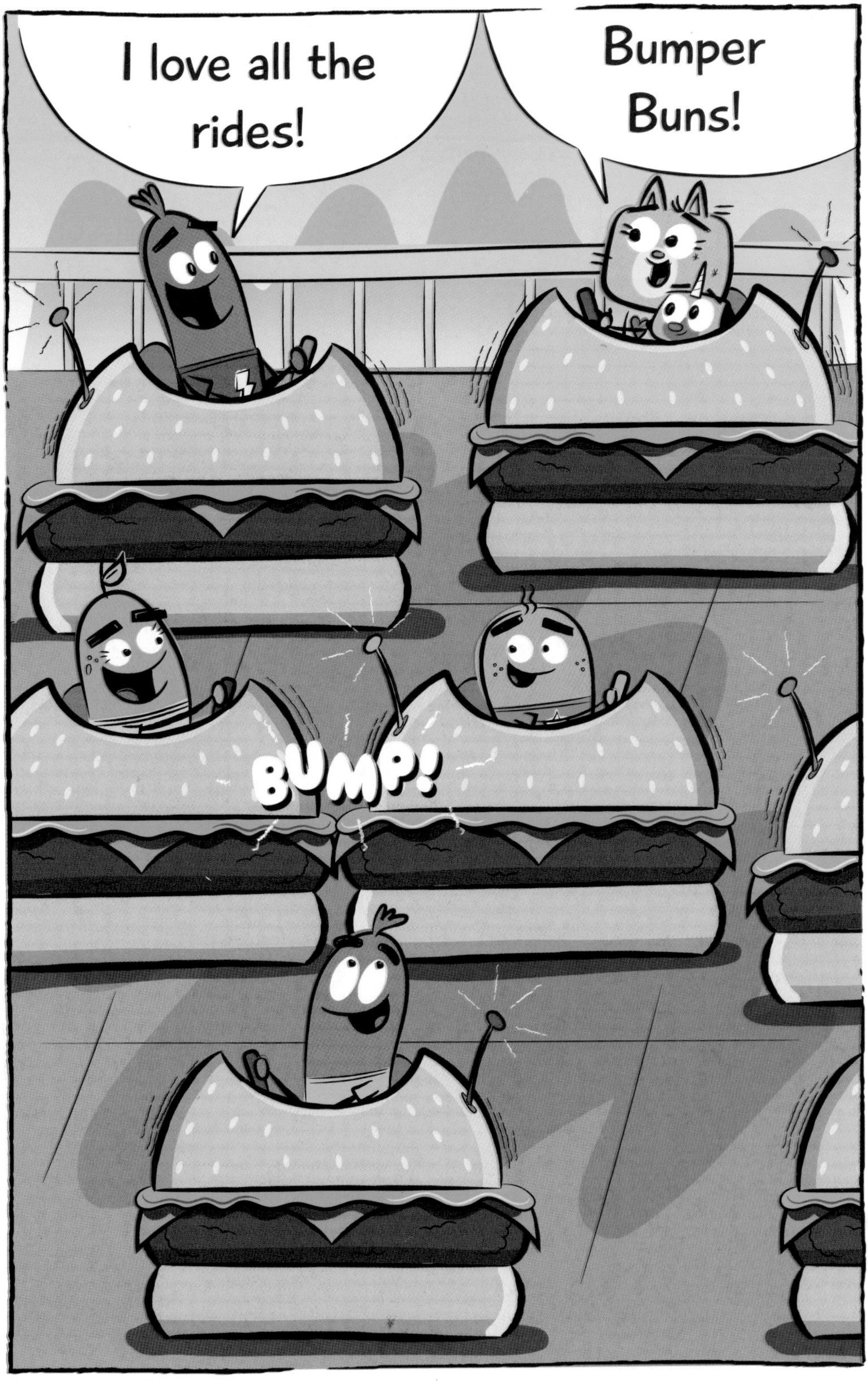
I love all the rides!
Bumper Buns!
BUMP!

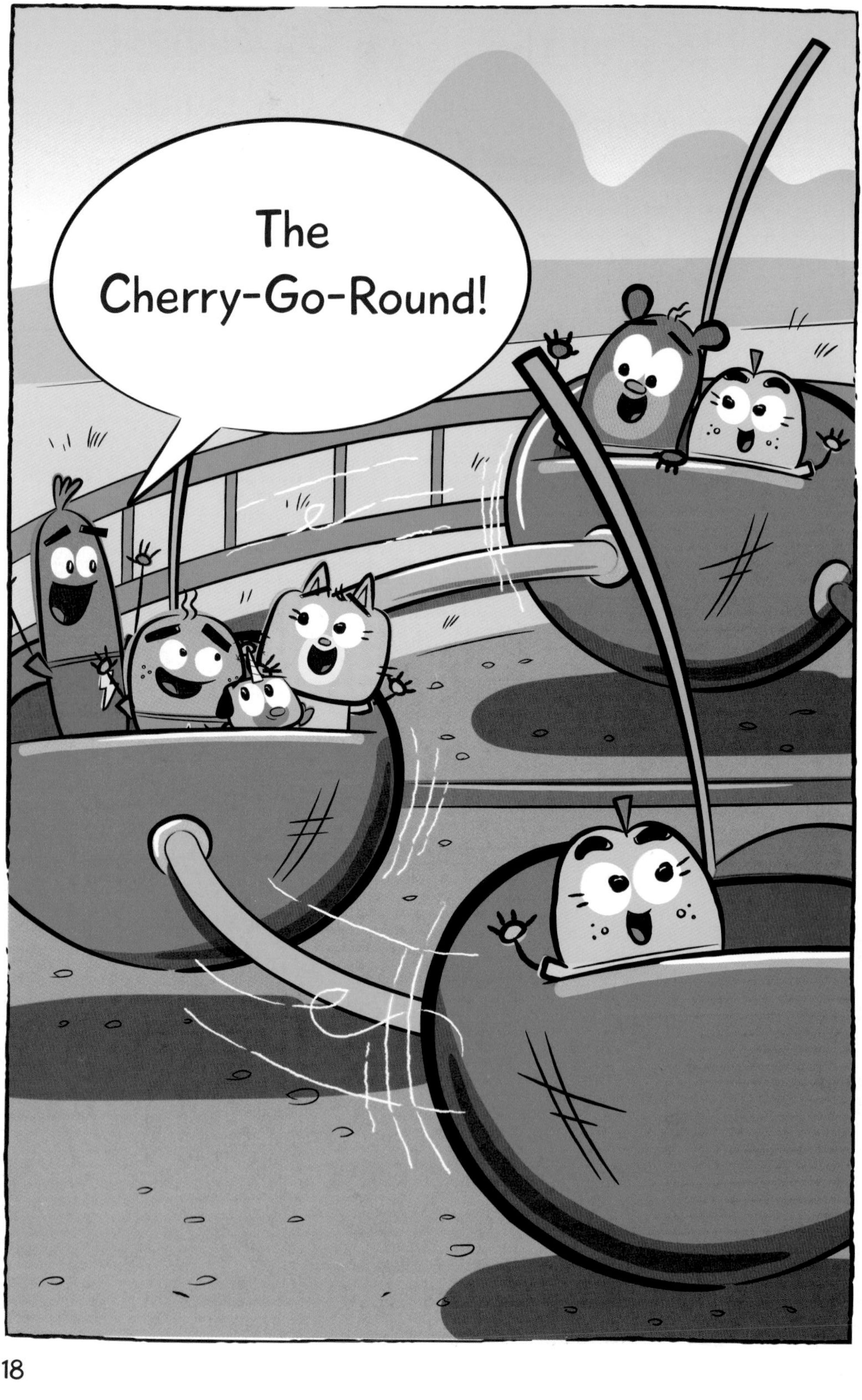
The Cherry-Go-Round!

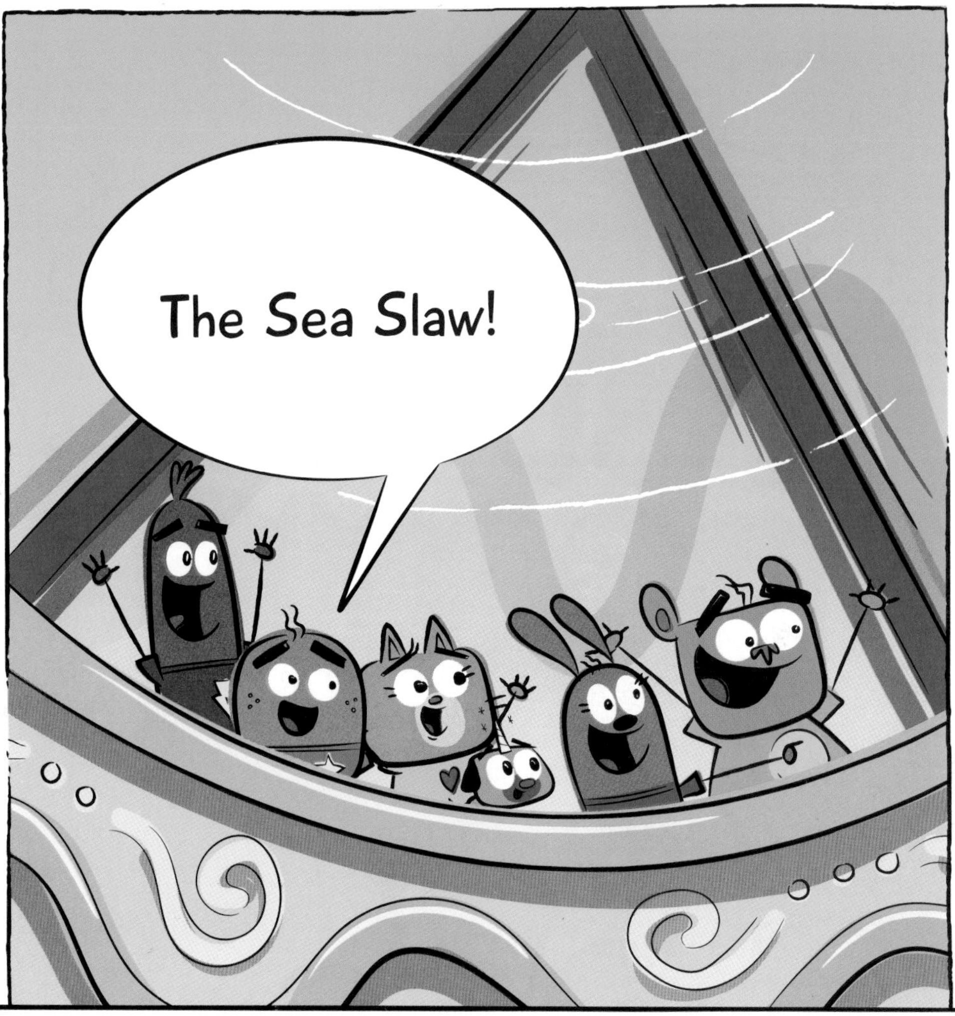
The Sea Slaw!

YUM FEST IS THE BEST!

Chapter 4

KETTLE BEANS

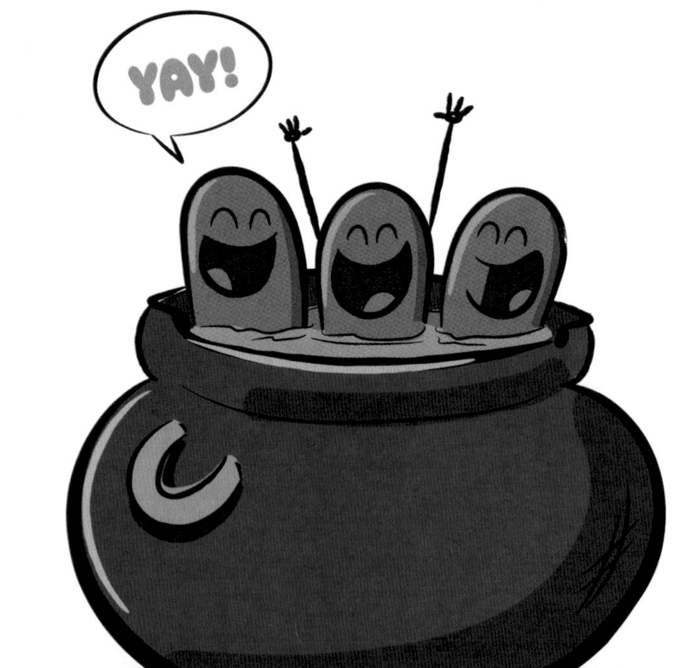
YAY!

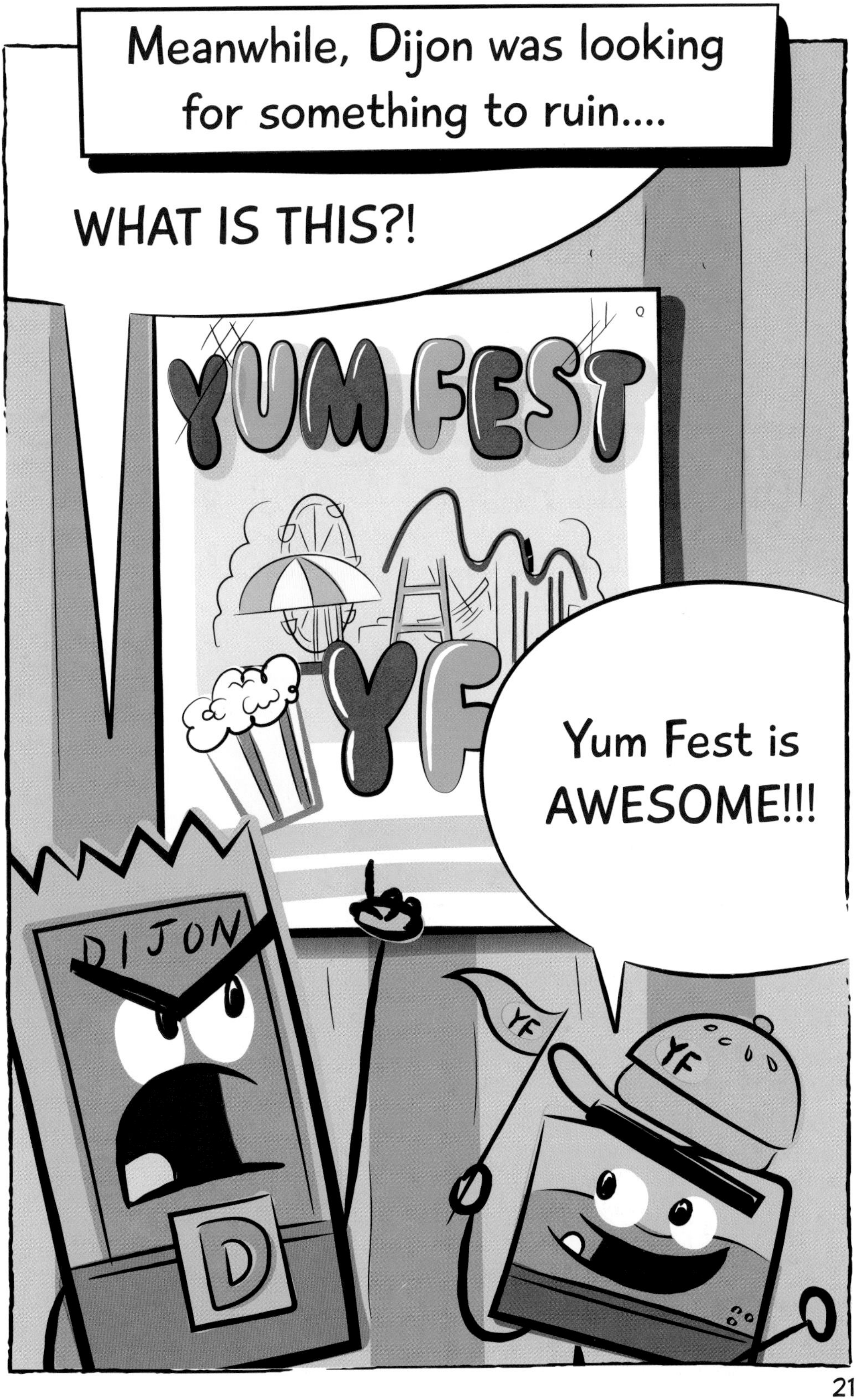
Meanwhile, Dijon was looking for something to ruin....
WHAT IS THIS?!
YUM FEST
YF
Yum Fest is AWESOME!!!
DIJON
D
YF
YF

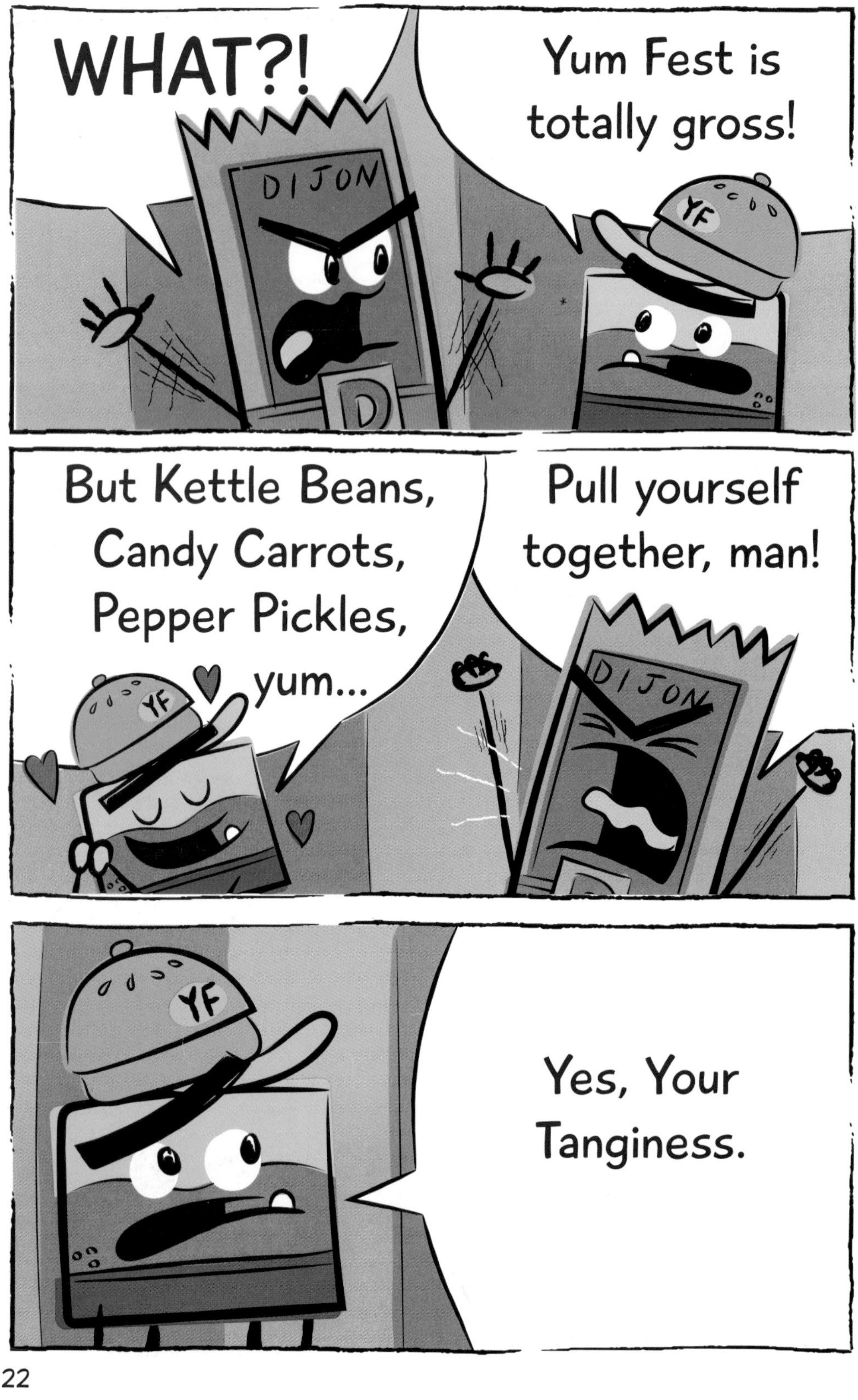
WHAT?!
Yum Fest is totally gross!
DIJON
YF
But Kettle Beans, Candy Carrots, Pepper Pickles, yum...
Pull yourself together, man!
DIJON
YF
Yes, Your Tanginess.

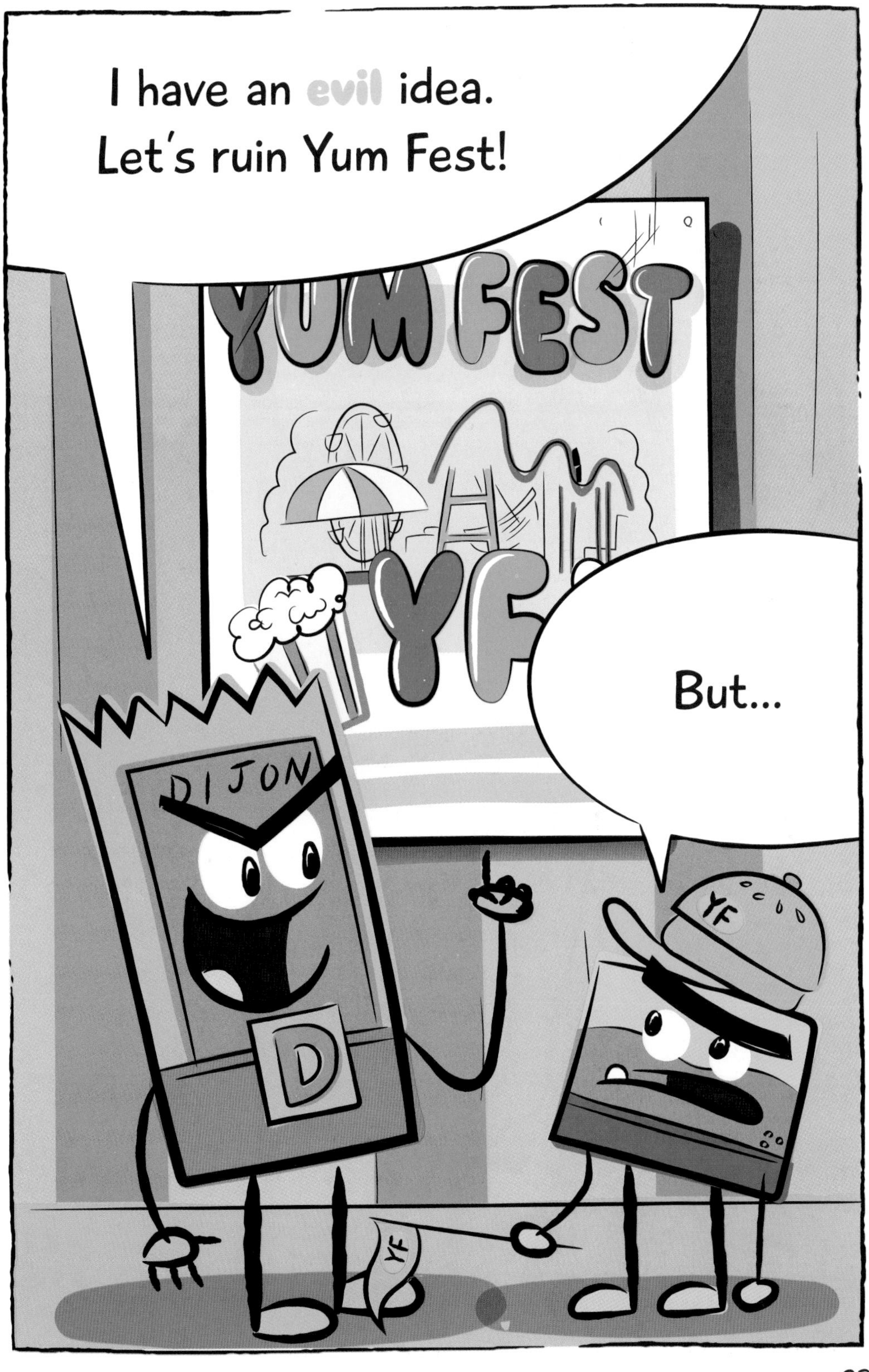
I have an evil idea.
Let's ruin Yum Fest!
YUM FEST
YF
DIJON
D
But...
YF
YF

Chapter 5

MAD YUMMY

DIJON
D

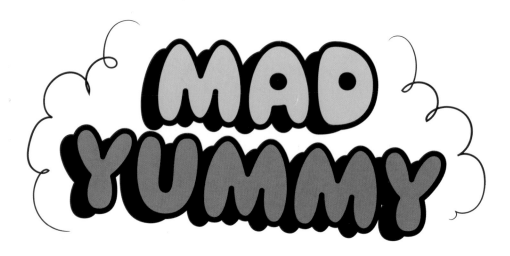

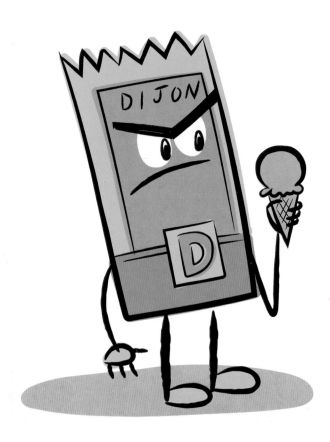

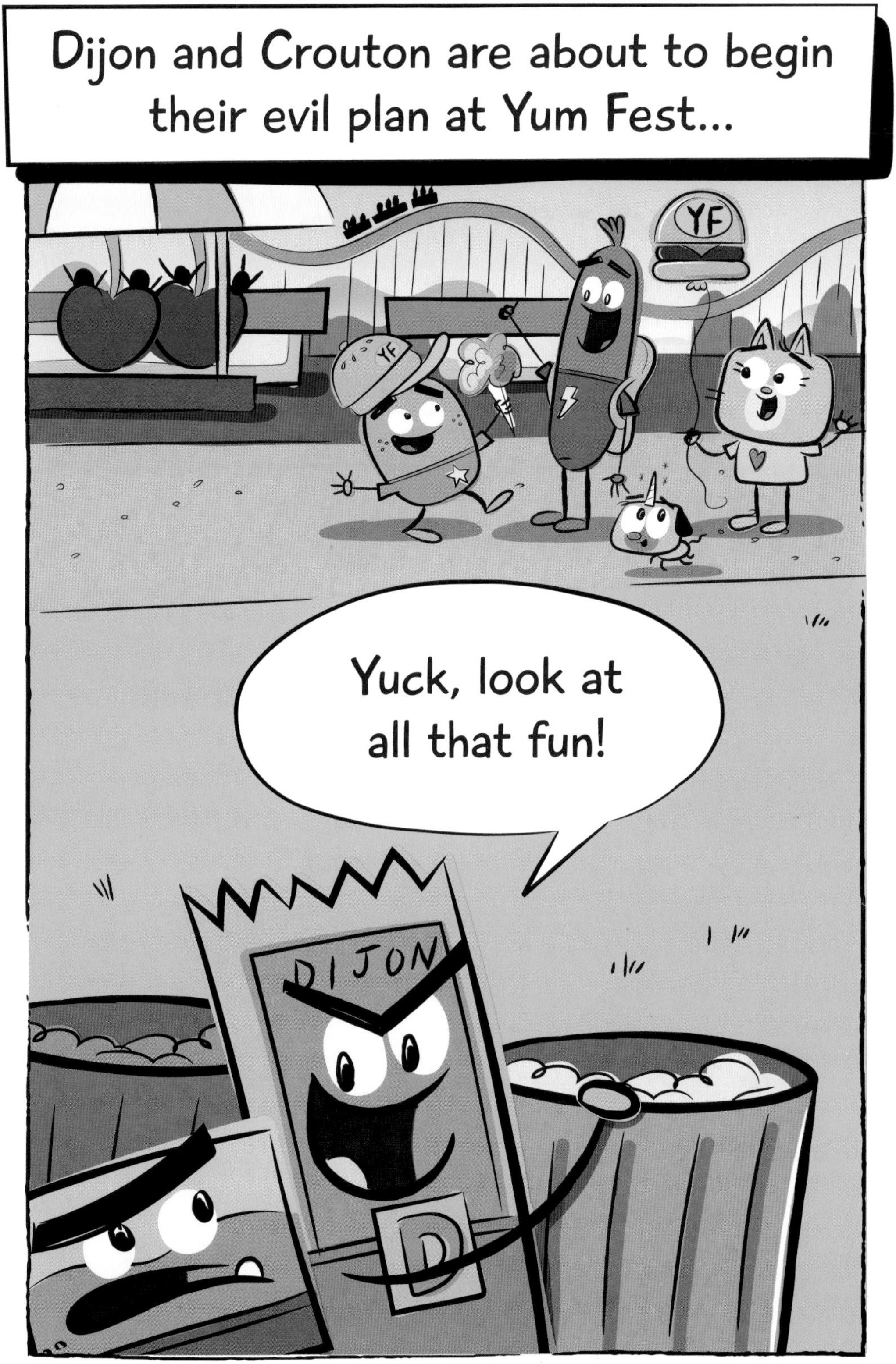
Dijon and Crouton are about to begin their evil plan at Yum Fest...
YF
Yuck, look at all that fun!
DIJON
D

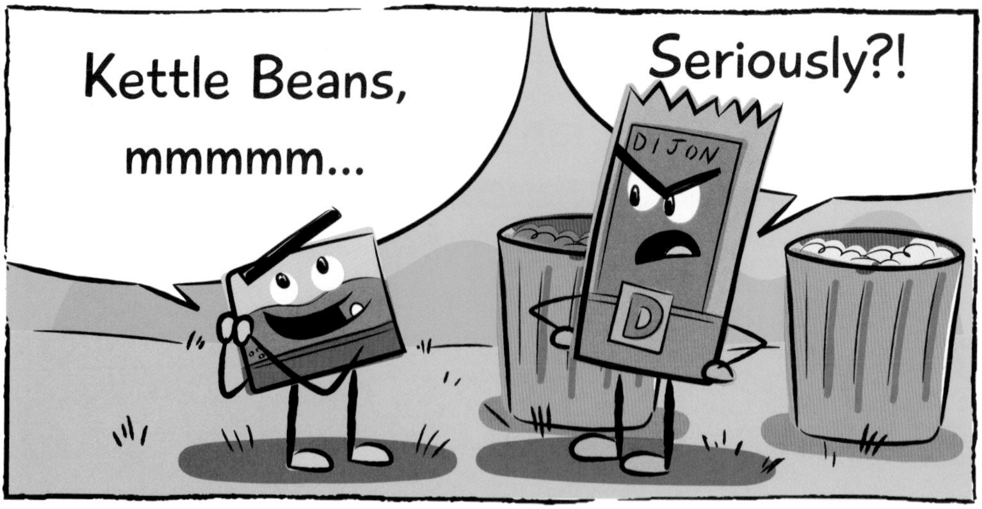
Kettle Beans,
mmmmm...
Seriously?!
DIJON
D

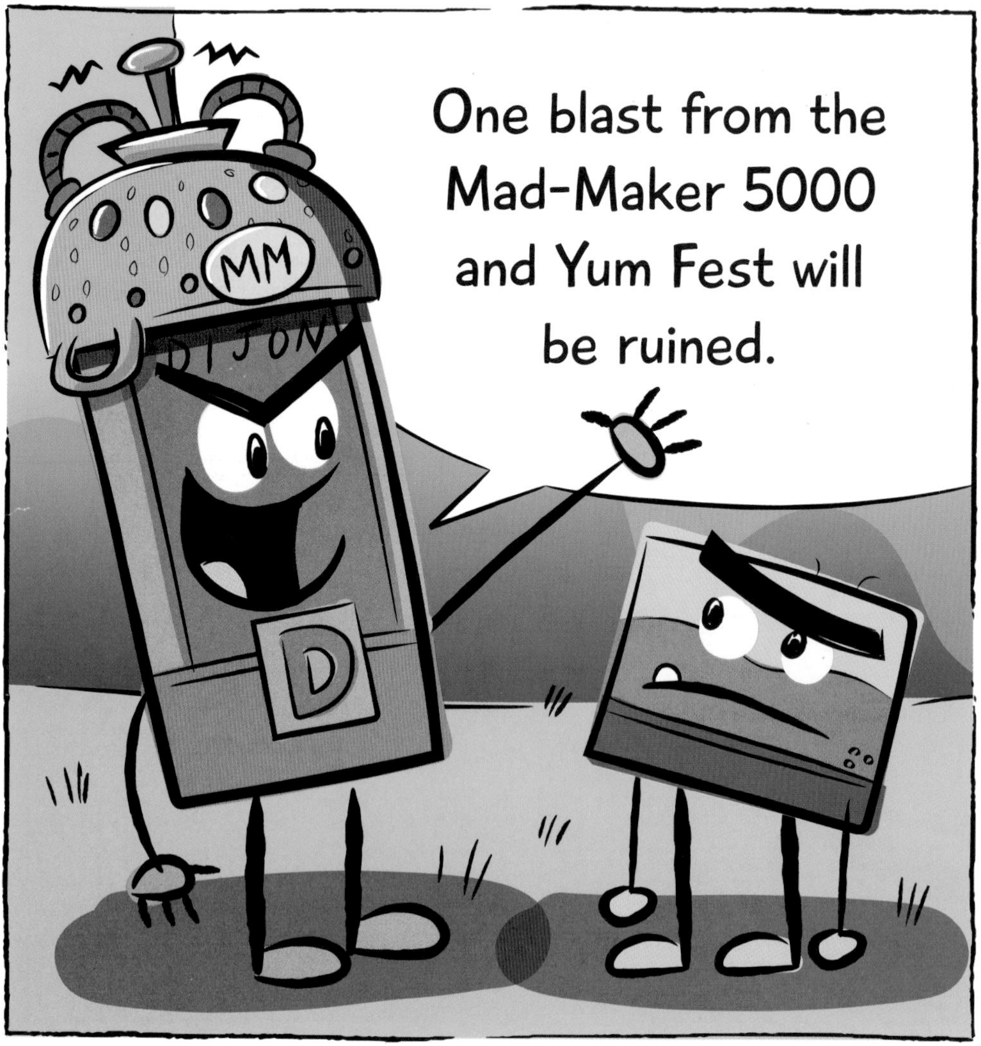
One blast from the
Mad-Maker 5000
and Yum Fest will
be ruined.
MM
DIJON
D

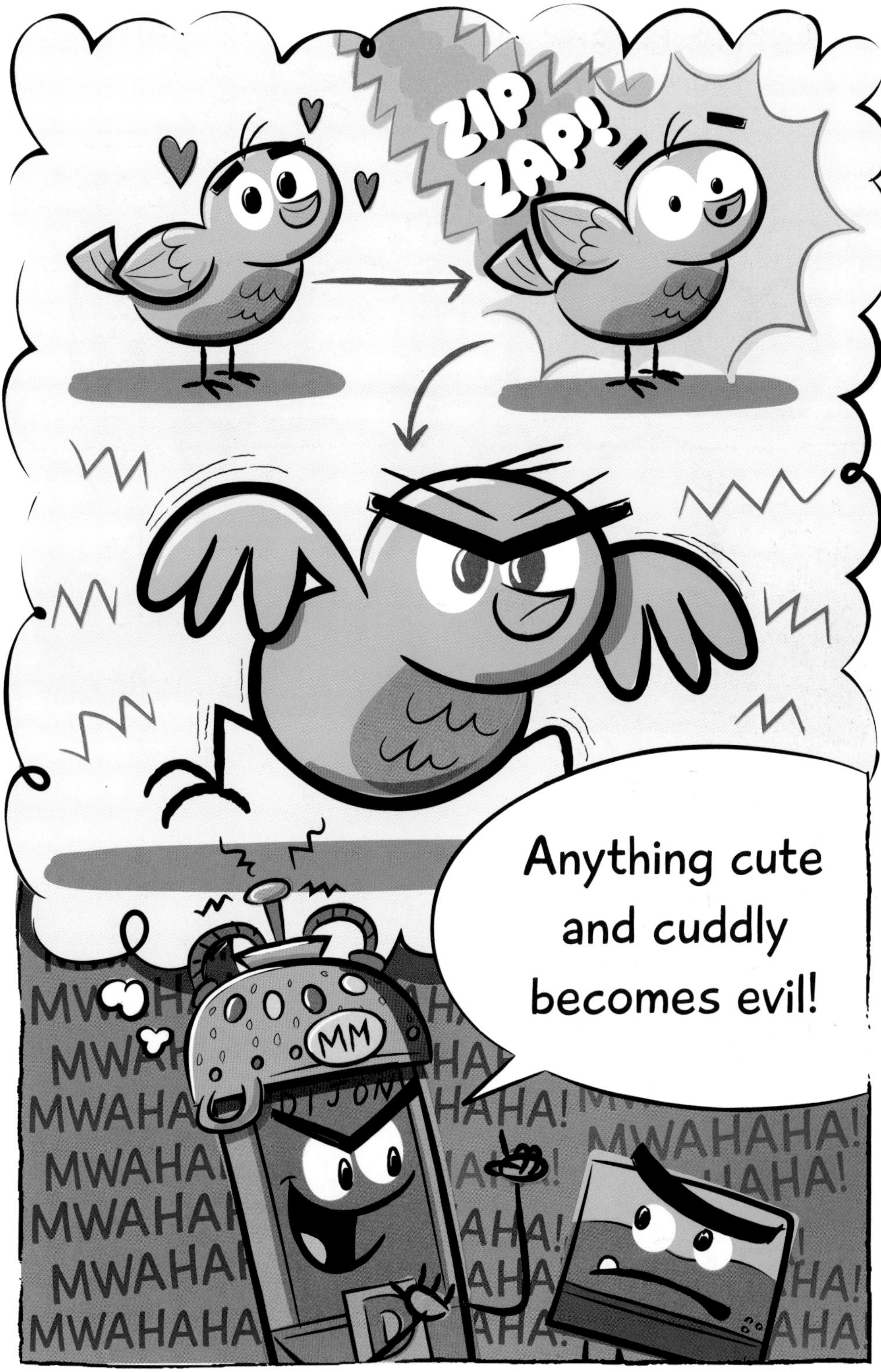
ZIP ZAP!
Anything cute and cuddly becomes evil!
MM
MWAHAHA! MWAHAHA! MWAHAHA! MWAHAHA! MWAHAHA! MWAHAHA! MWAHAHA!

Chapter 6

UNICORN PUPPY PROBLEM!

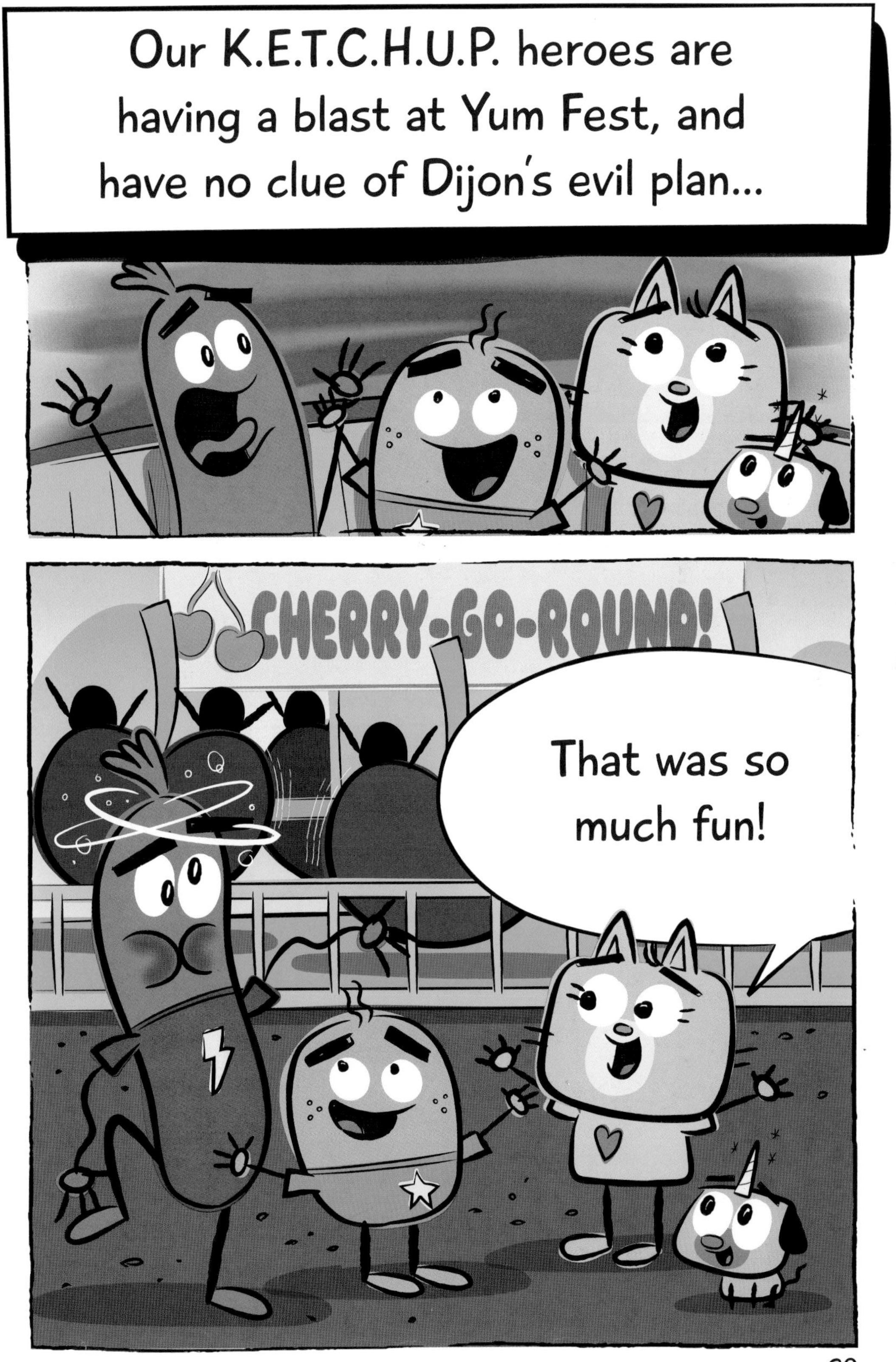
Our K.E.T.C.H.U.P. heroes are having a blast at Yum Fest, and have no clue of Dijon's evil plan...
CHERRY-GO-ROUND!
That was so much fun!

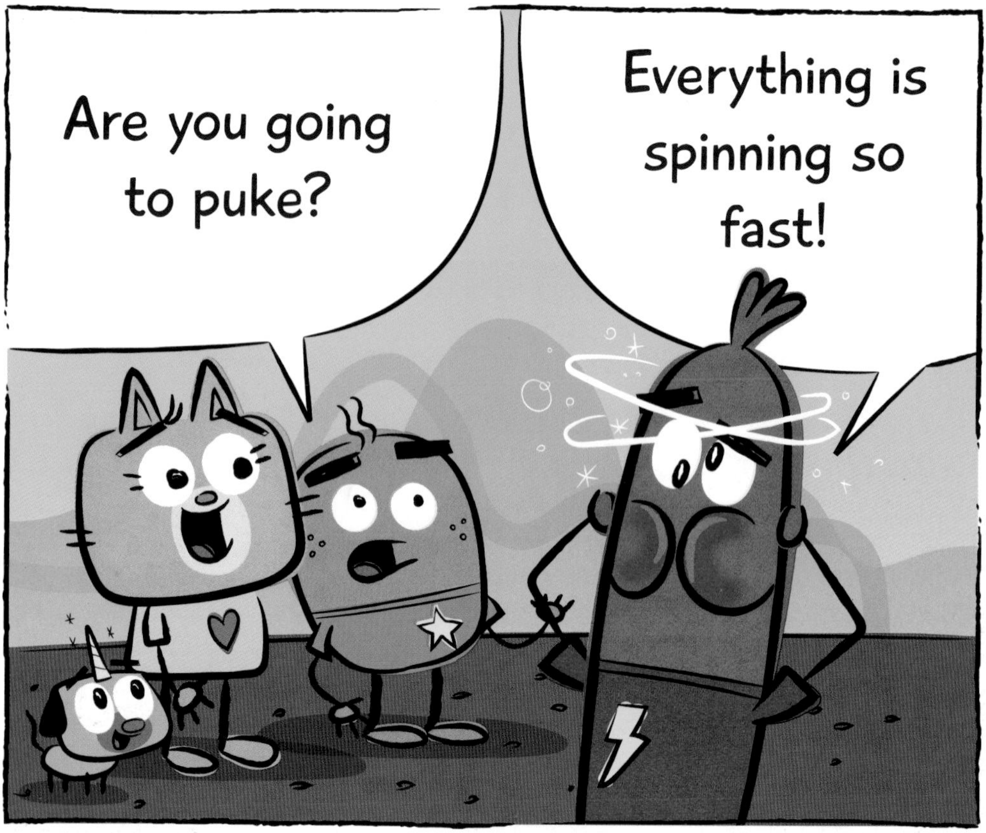
Are you going to puke?
Everything is spinning so fast!

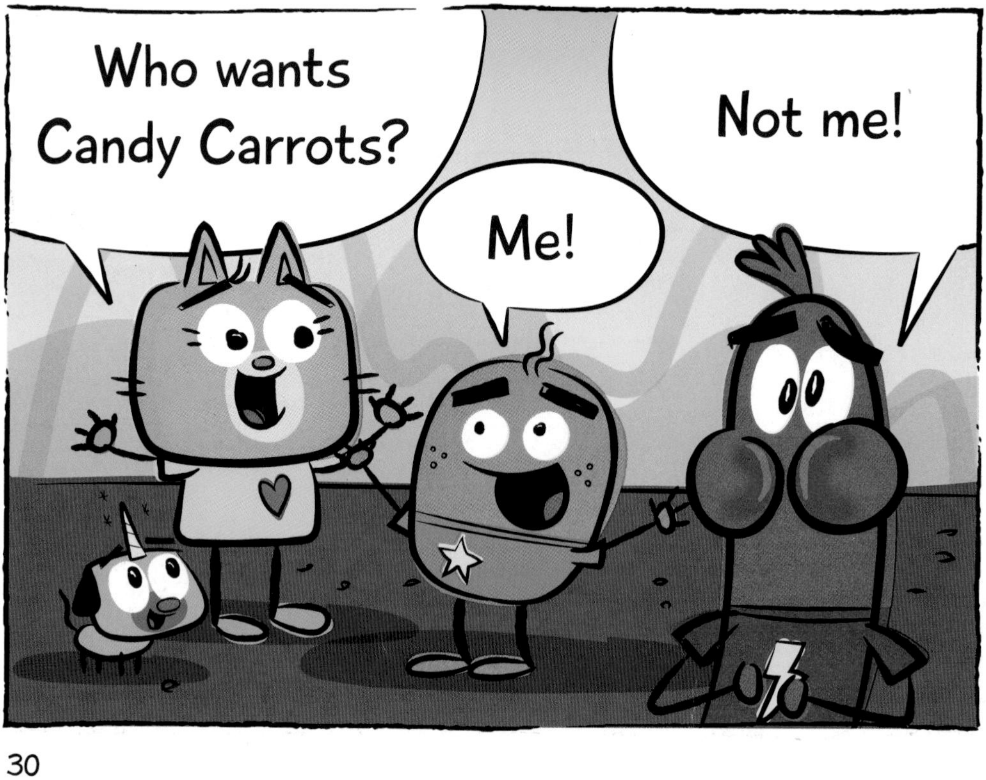
Who wants Candy Carrots?
Me!
Not me!

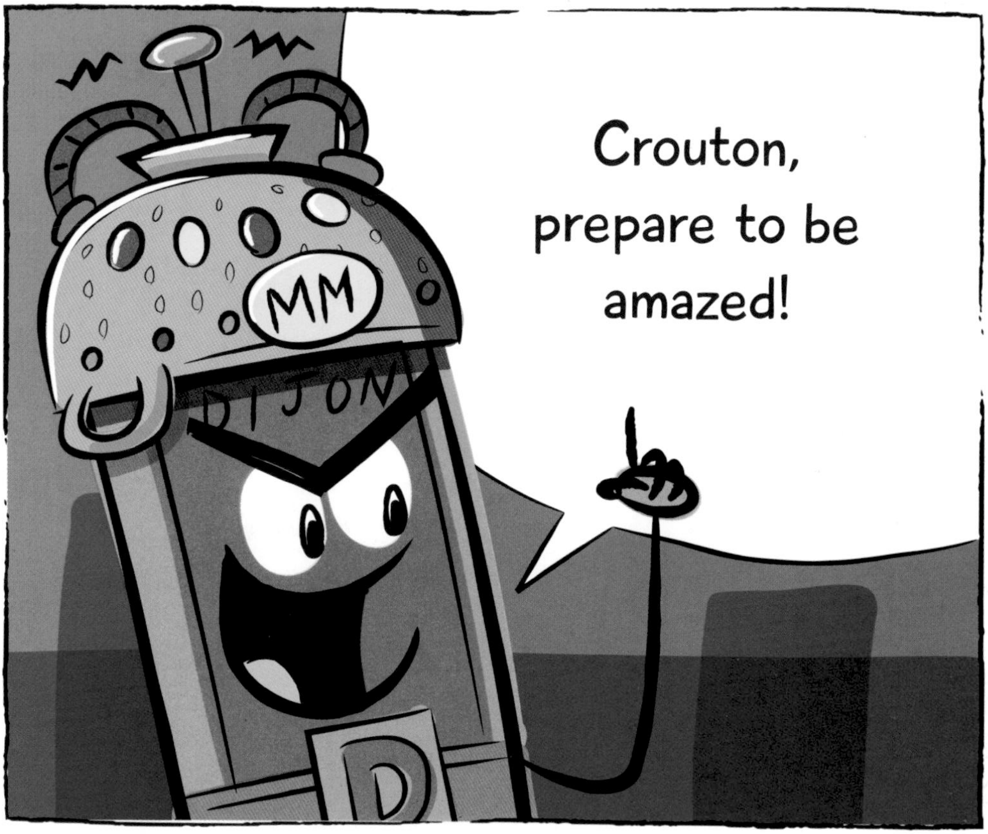
Crouton,
prepare to be
amazed!
MM
DIJON
D

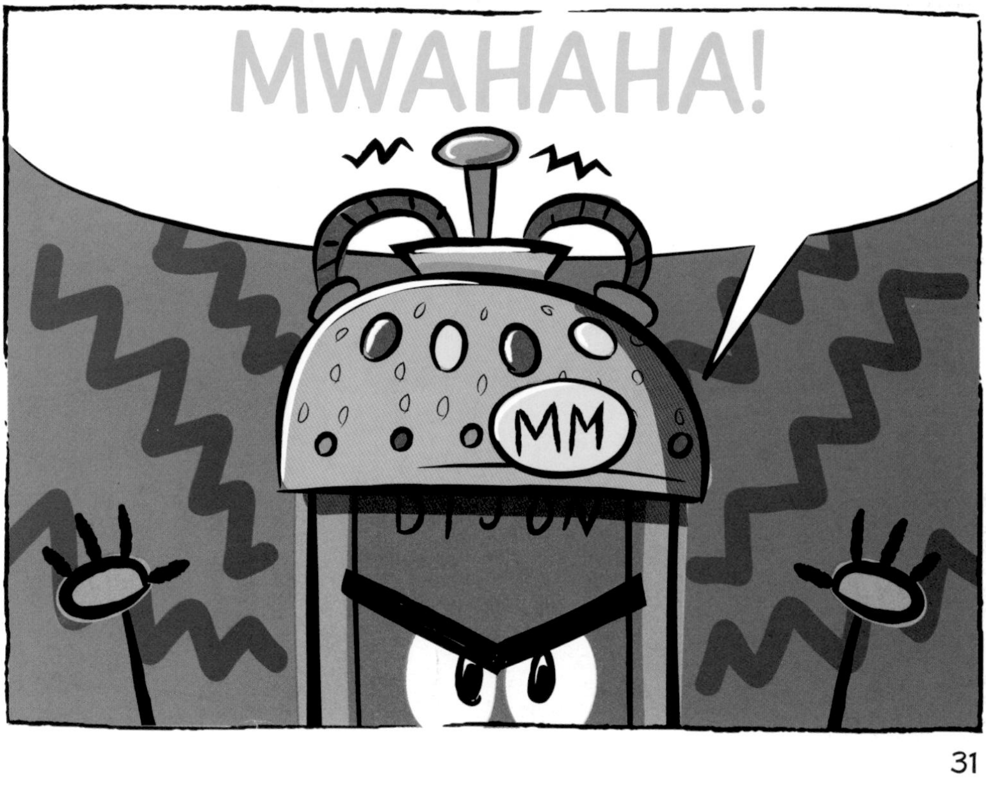
MWAHAHA!
MM

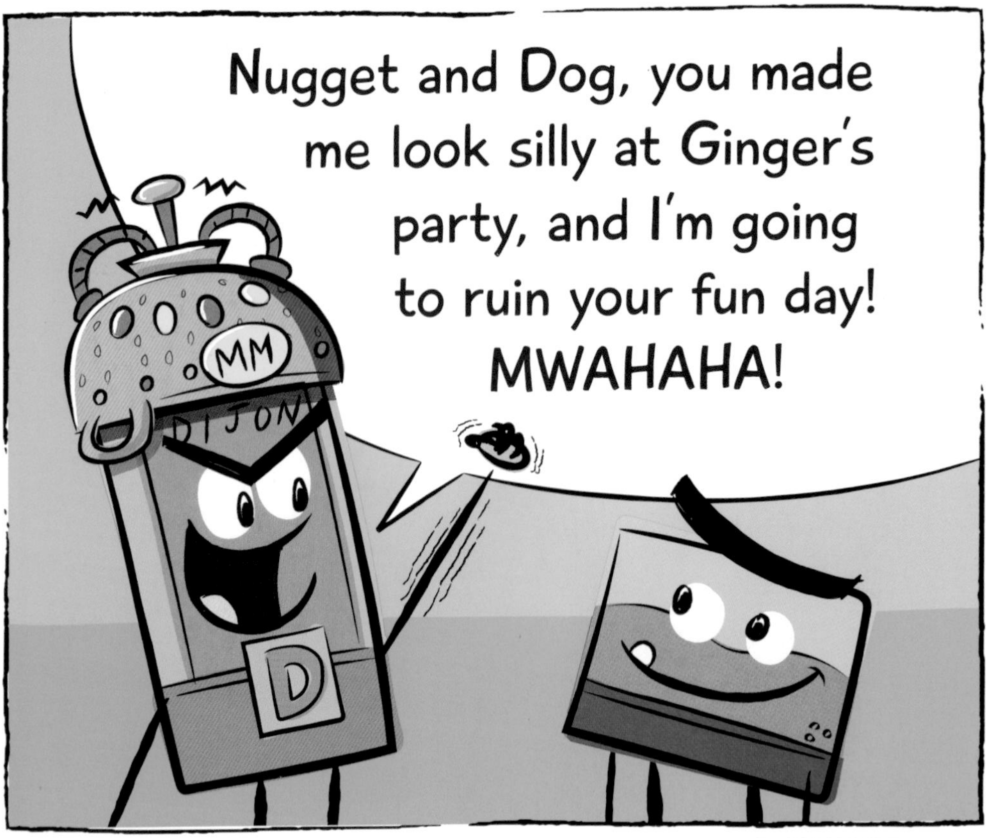
Nugget and Dog, you made me look silly at Ginger's party, and I'm going to ruin your fun day! MWAHAHA!
MM
DIJON
D

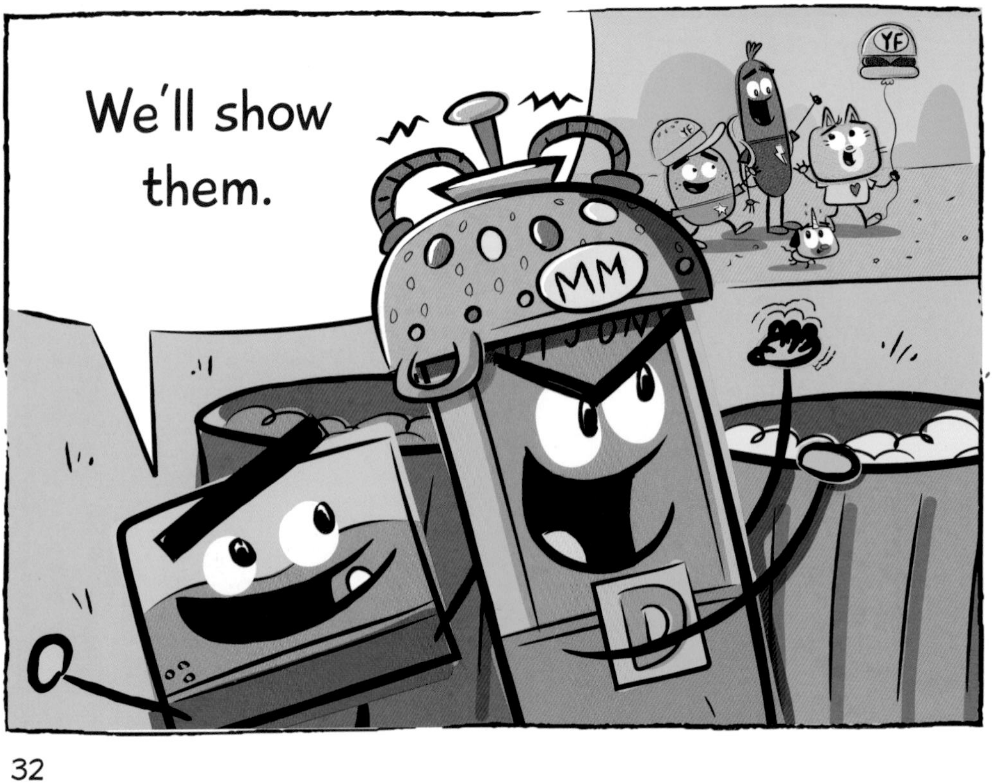
We'll show them.
YF
MM
D

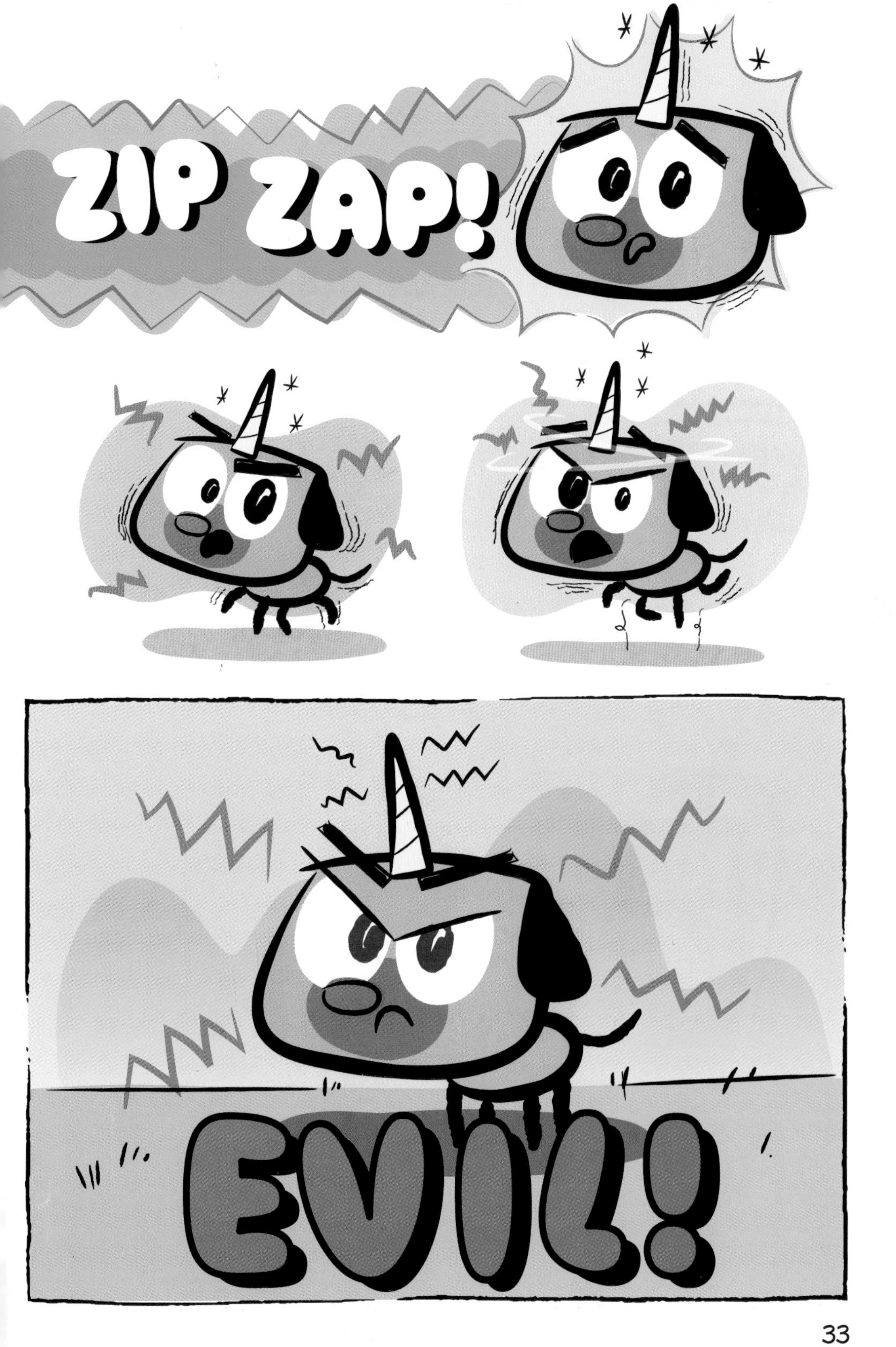
ZIP ZAP!
EVIL!

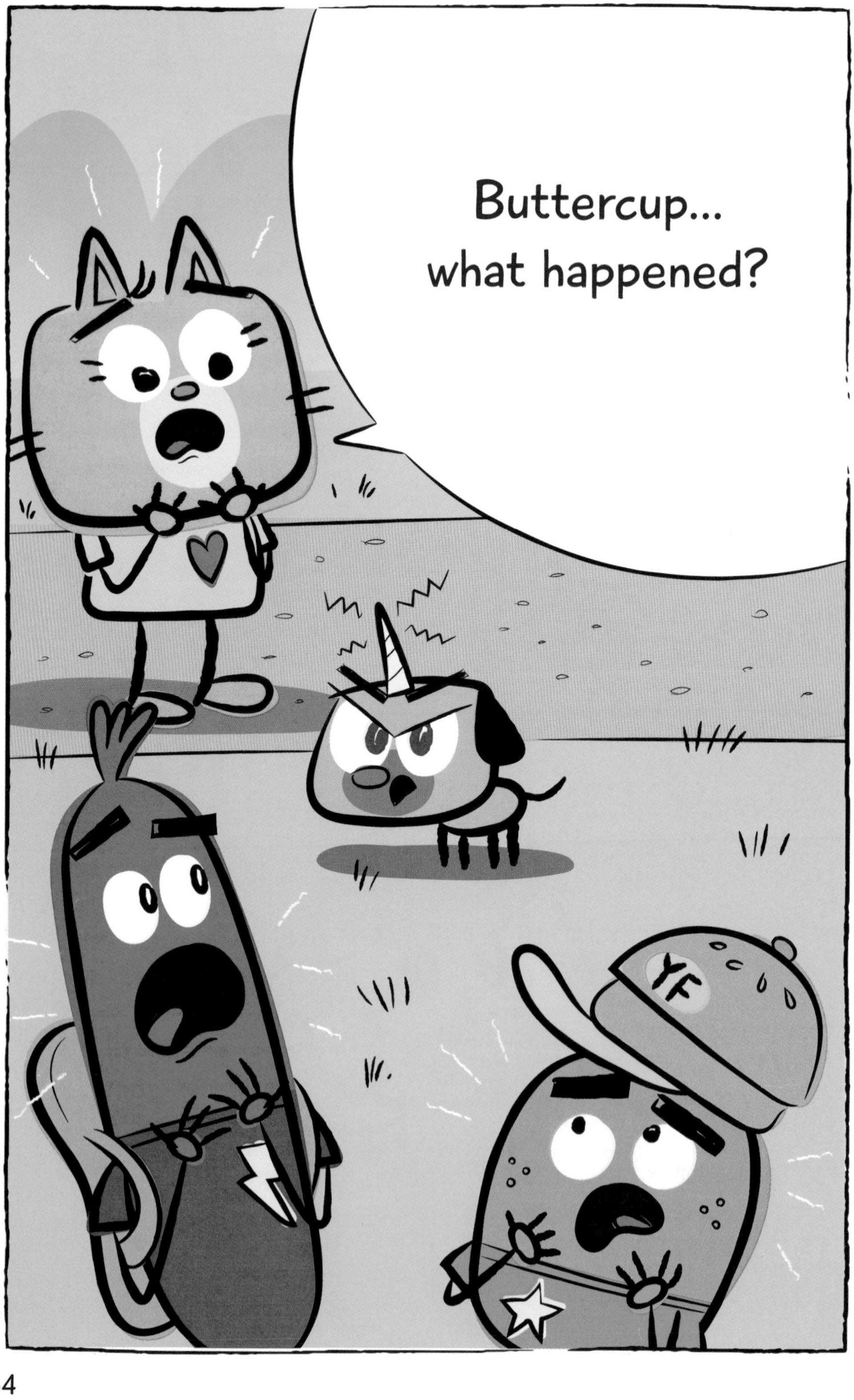
Buttercup...
what happened?
YF

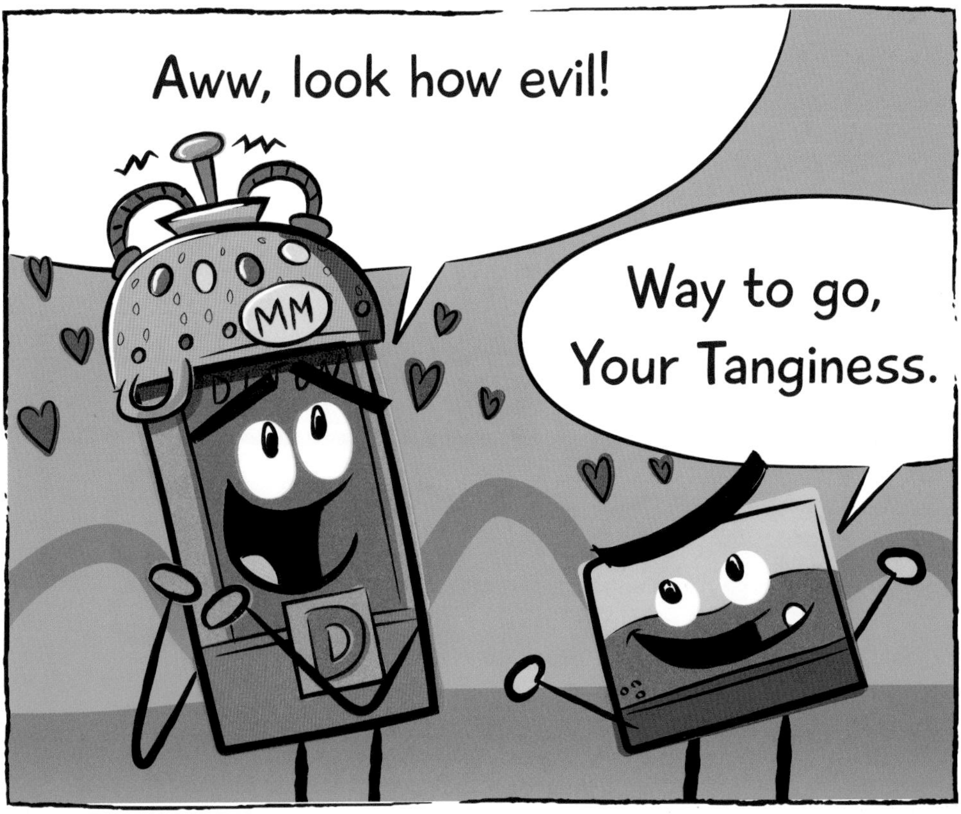
Aww, look how evil!
Way to go, Your Tanginess.
MM
D

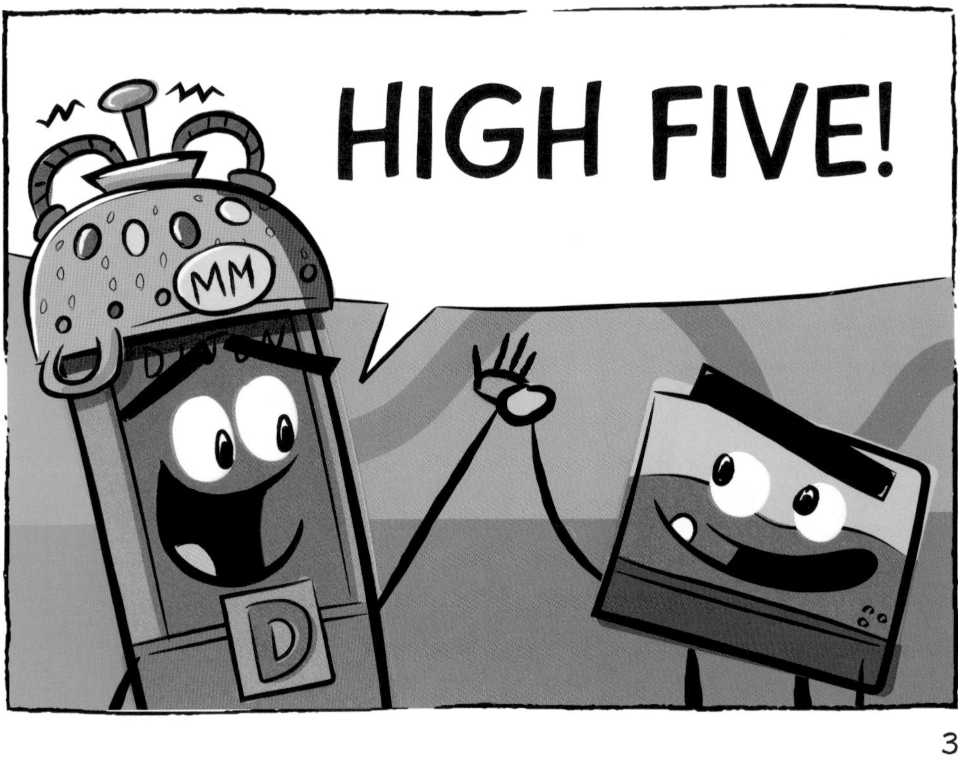
HIGH FIVE!
MM
D

Chapter 7

EVERYTHING'S CORNY!

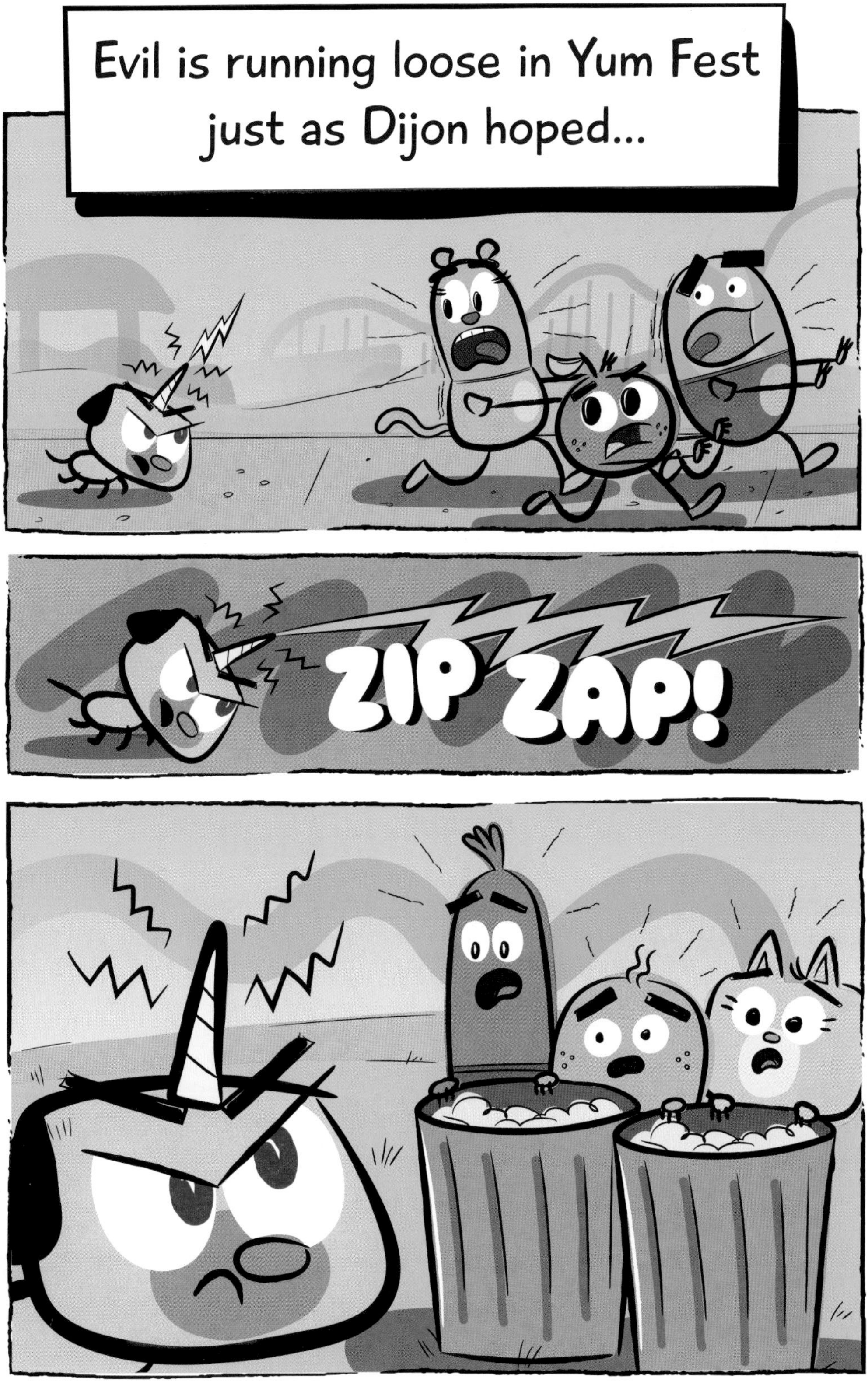
Evil is running loose in Yum Fest just as Dijon hoped...
ZIP ZAP!

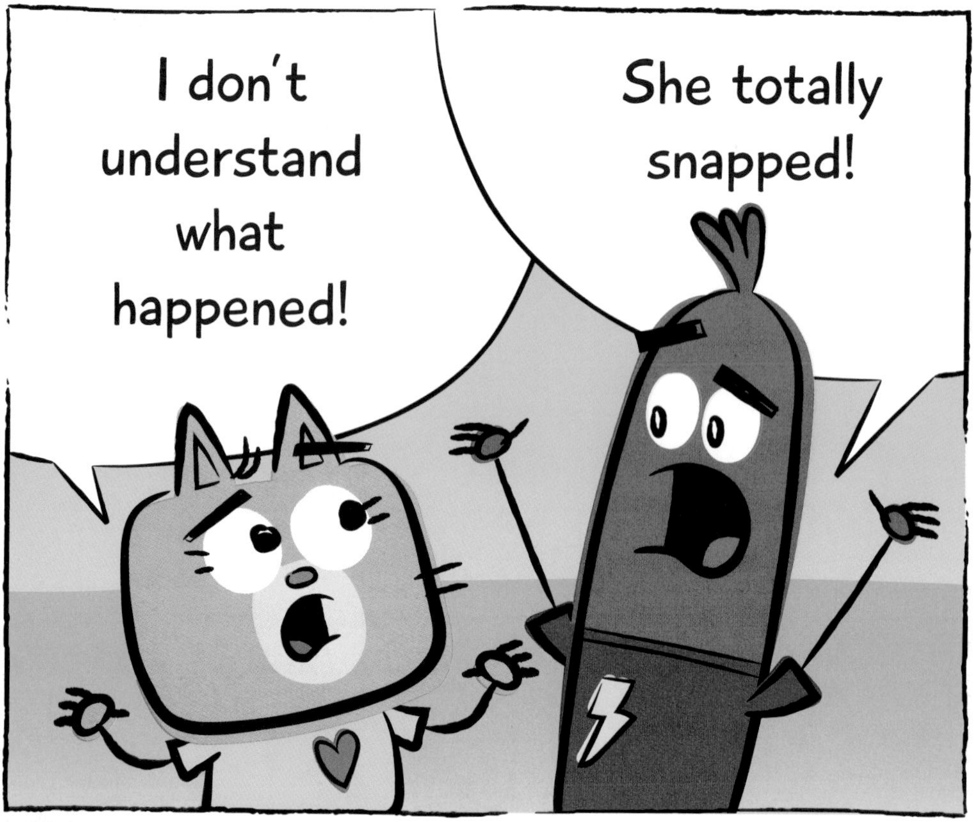
I don't understand what happened!
She totally snapped!

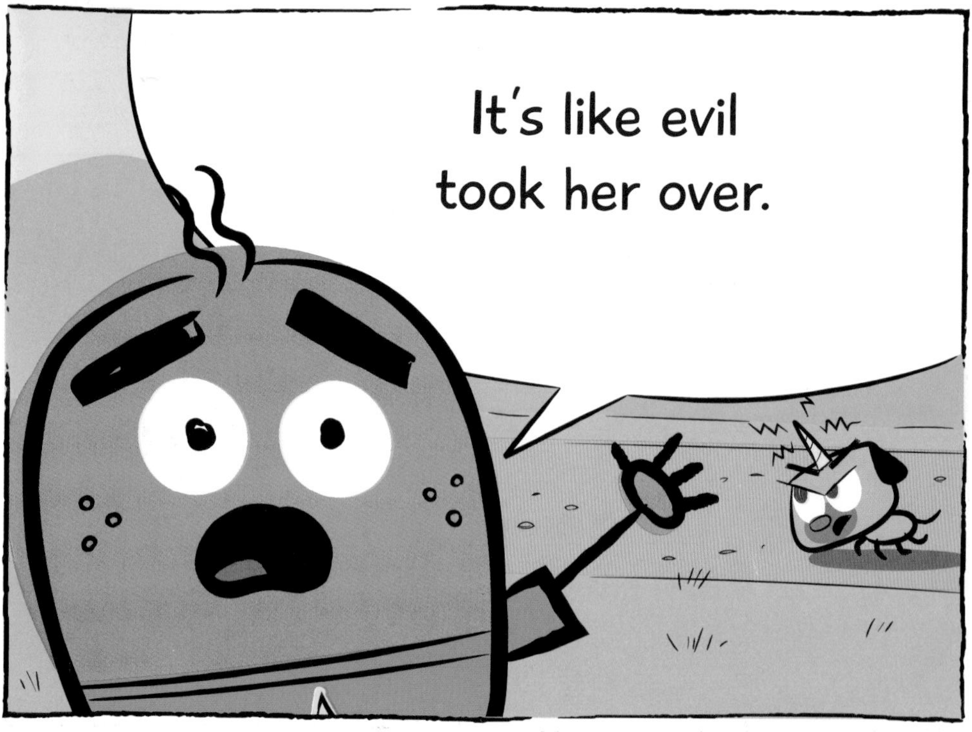
It's like evil took her over.

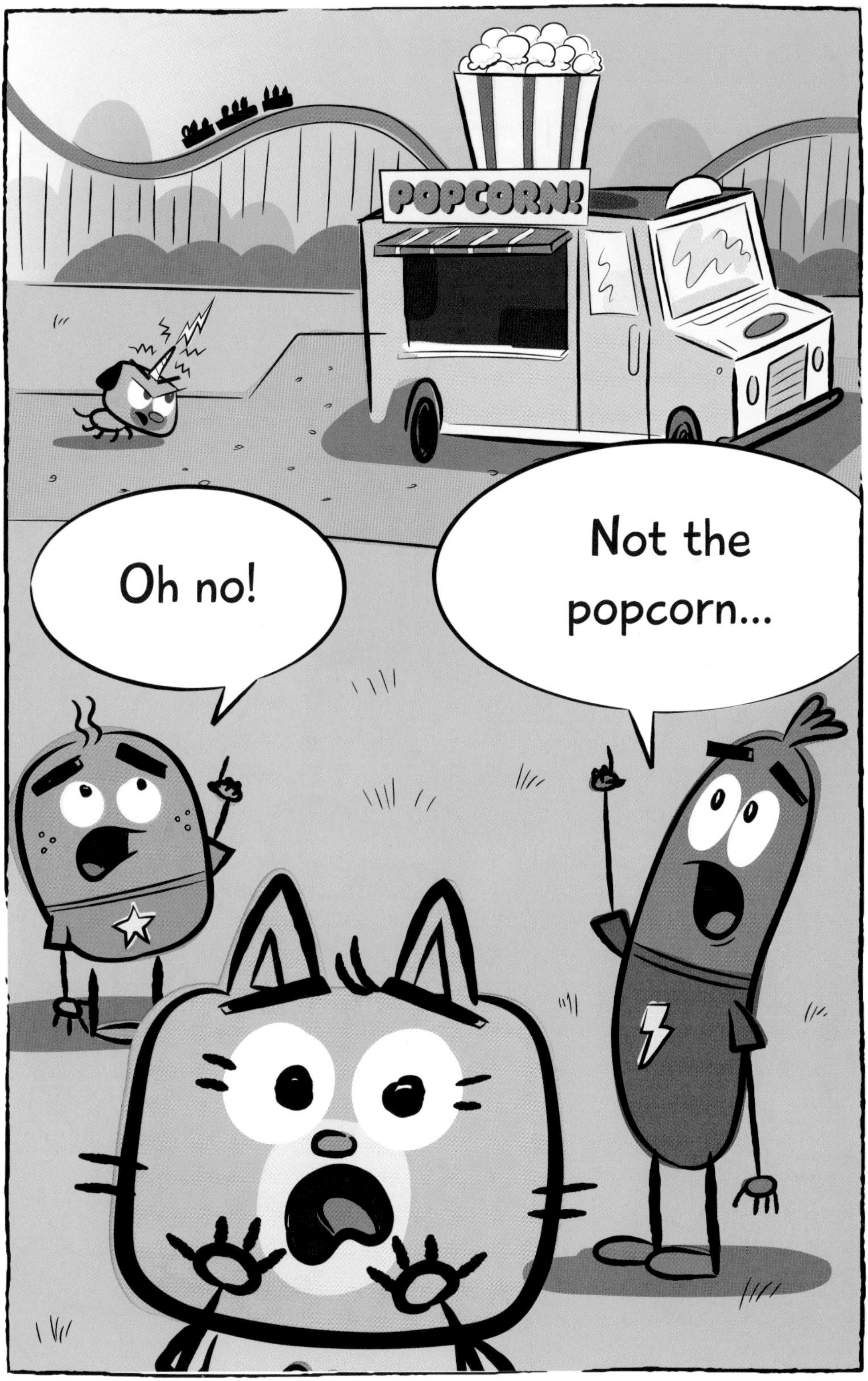
POPCORN!
Oh no!
Not the popcorn...

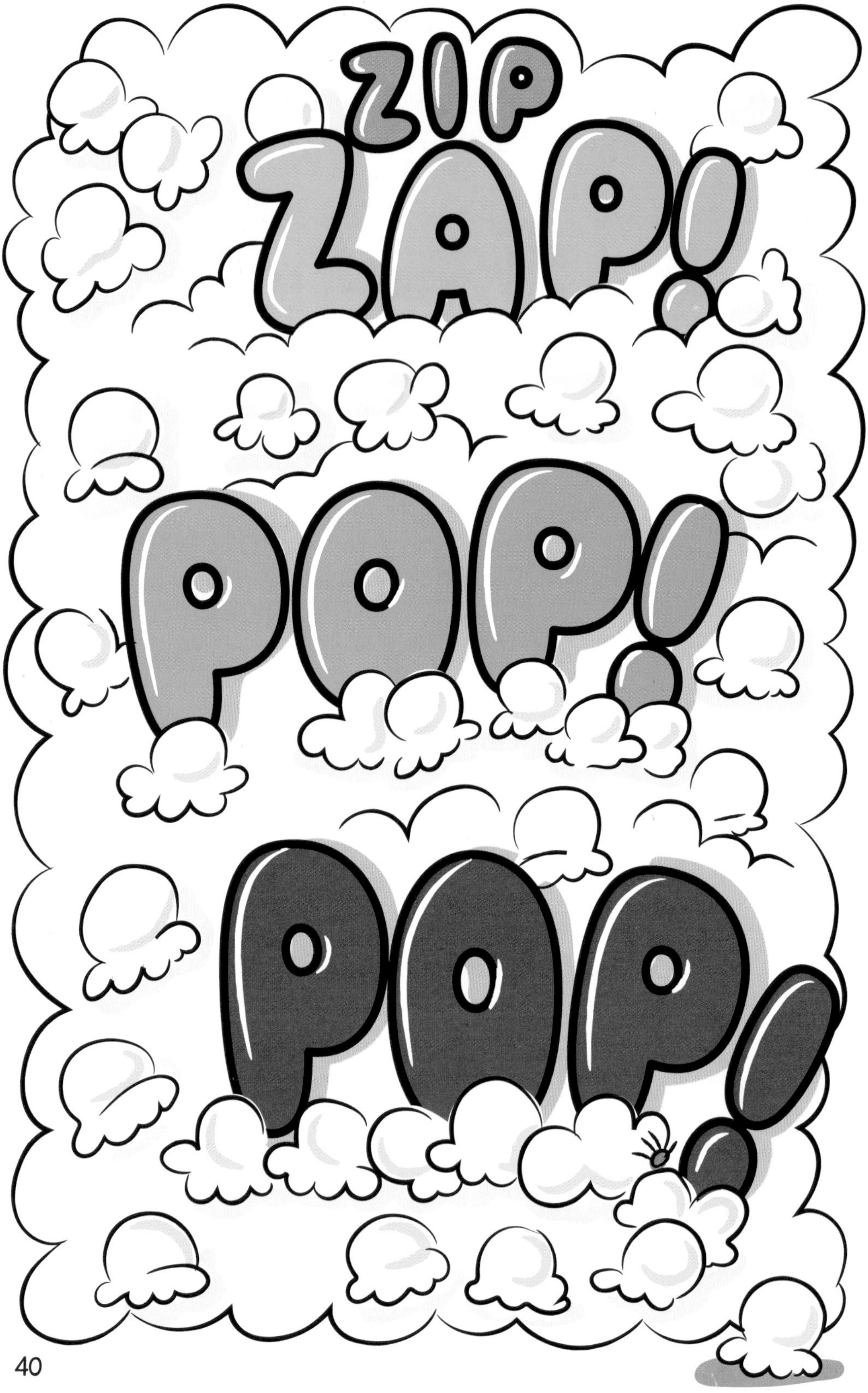
ZIP
ZAP!
POP!
POP!

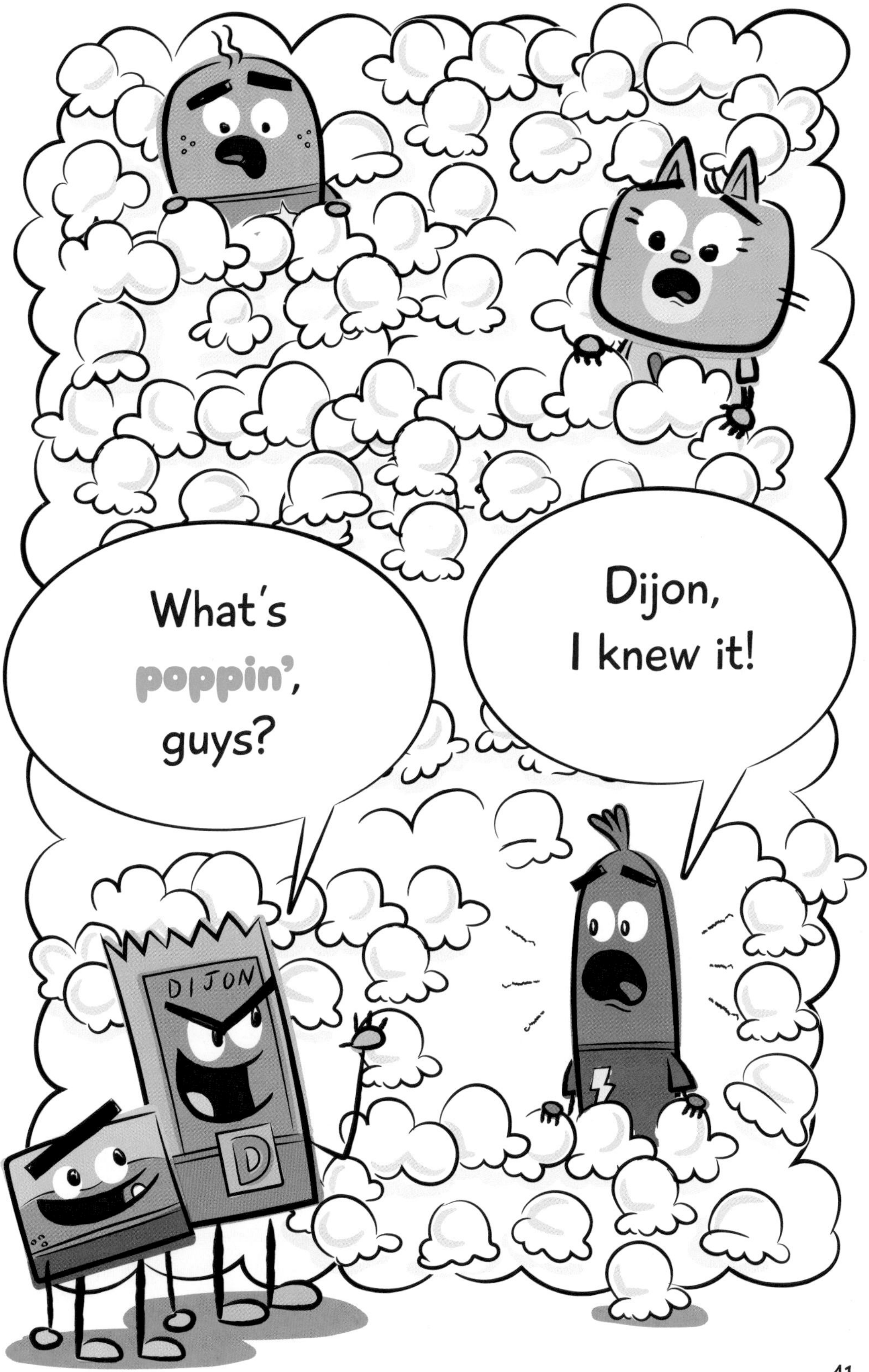
What's poppin', guys?
Dijon, I knew it!
DIJON
D

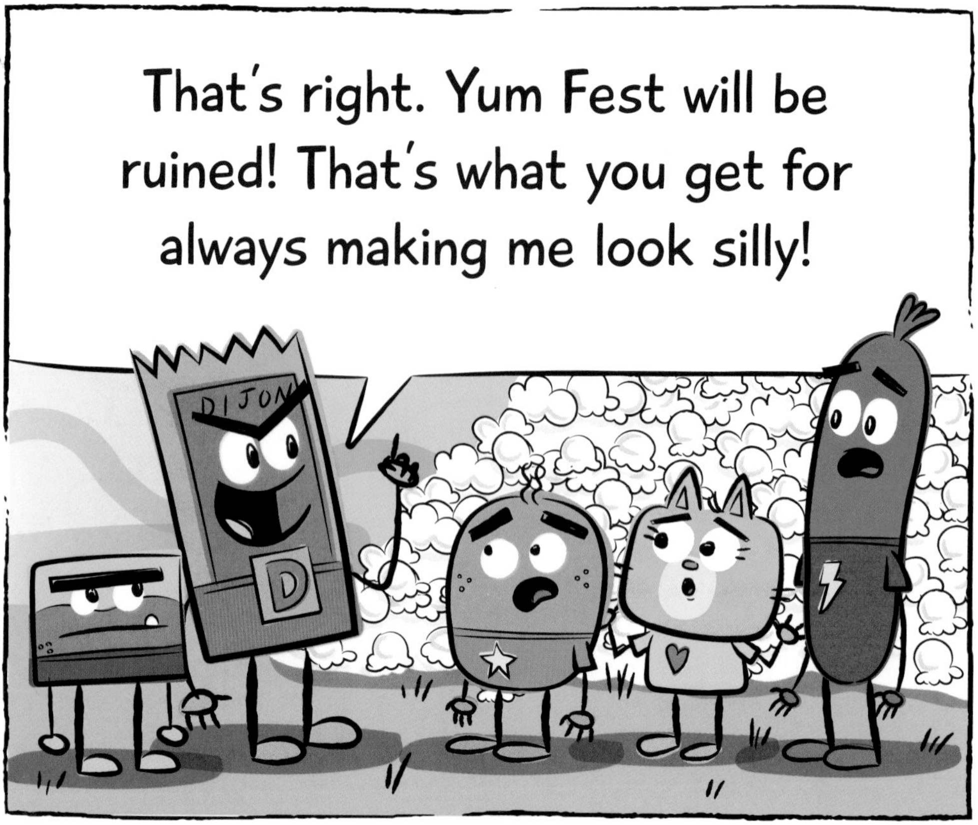
That's right. Yum Fest will be ruined! That's what you get for always making me look silly!
DIJON
D

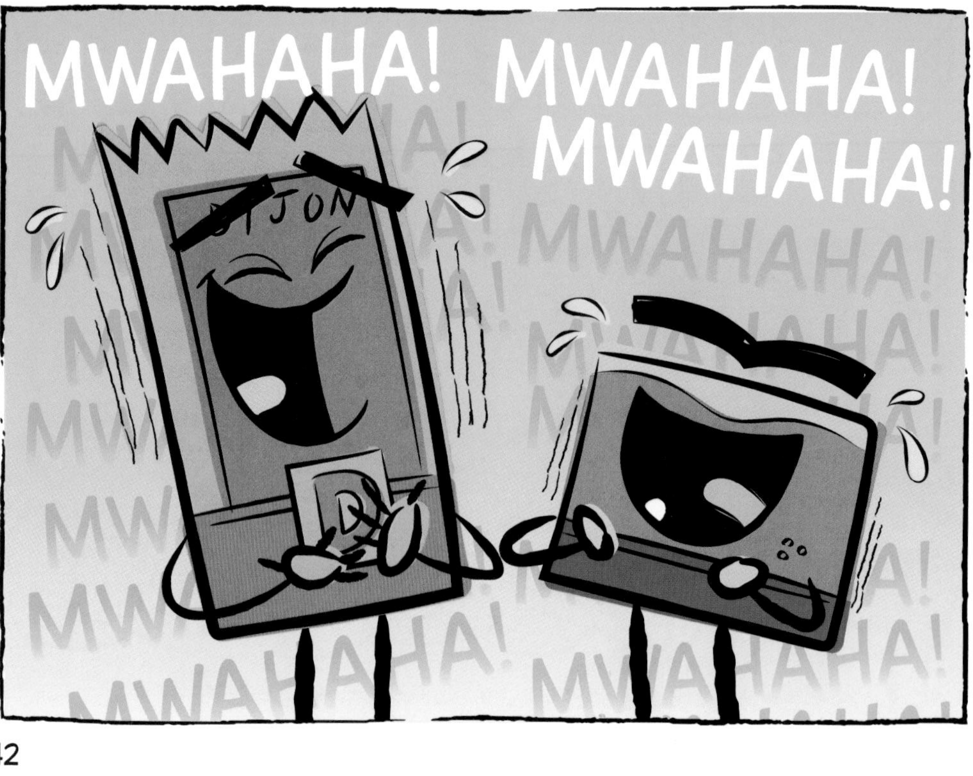
MWAHAHA! MWAHAHA!
MWAHAHA!
DIJON
D

Chapter 8
BITTER BUTTERCUP!

Just when Dijon thinks he has won, **K.E.T.C.H.U.P.** springs into action...

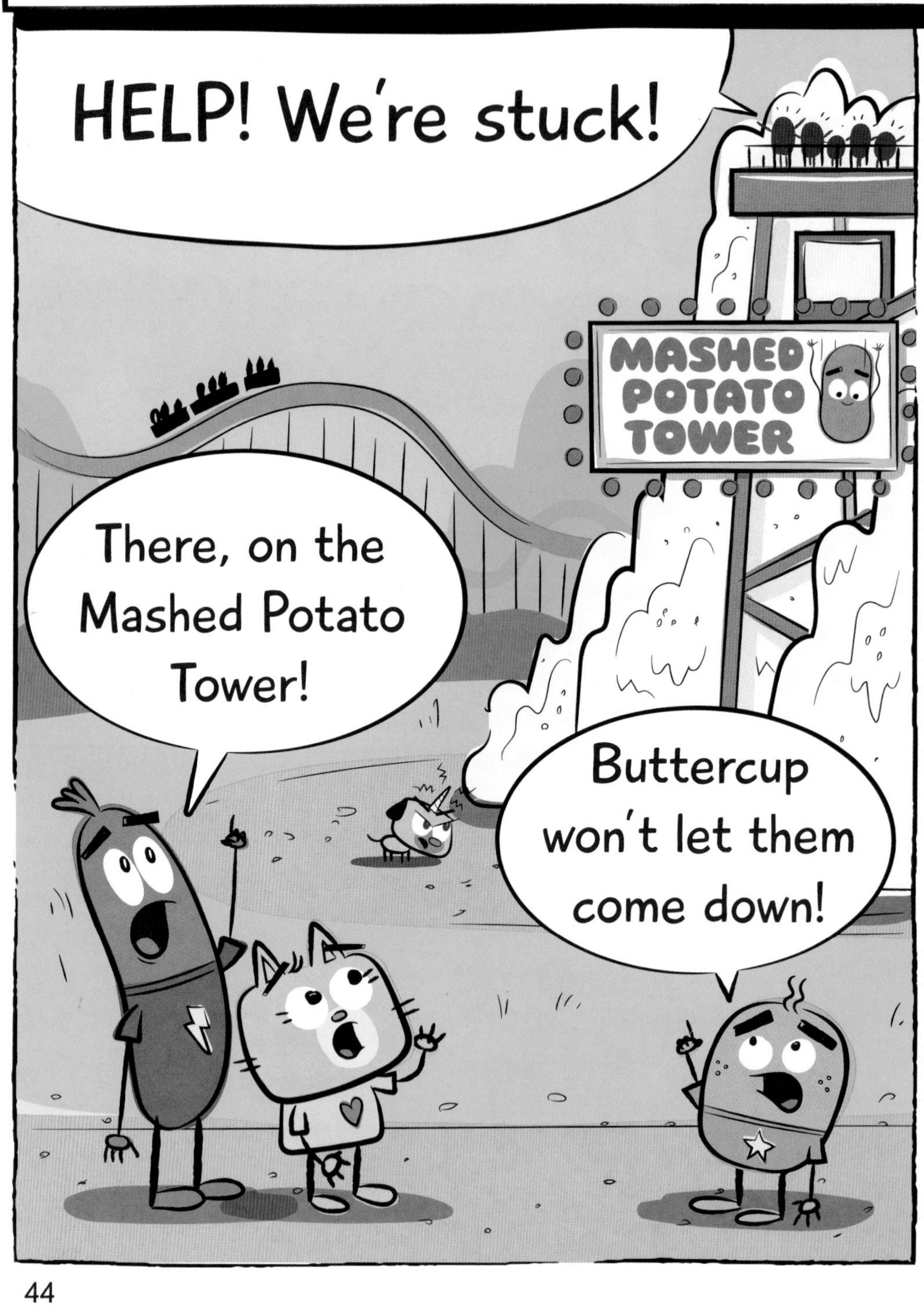
HELP! We're stuck!
MASHED POTATO TOWER
There, on the Mashed Potato Tower!
Buttercup won't let them come down!

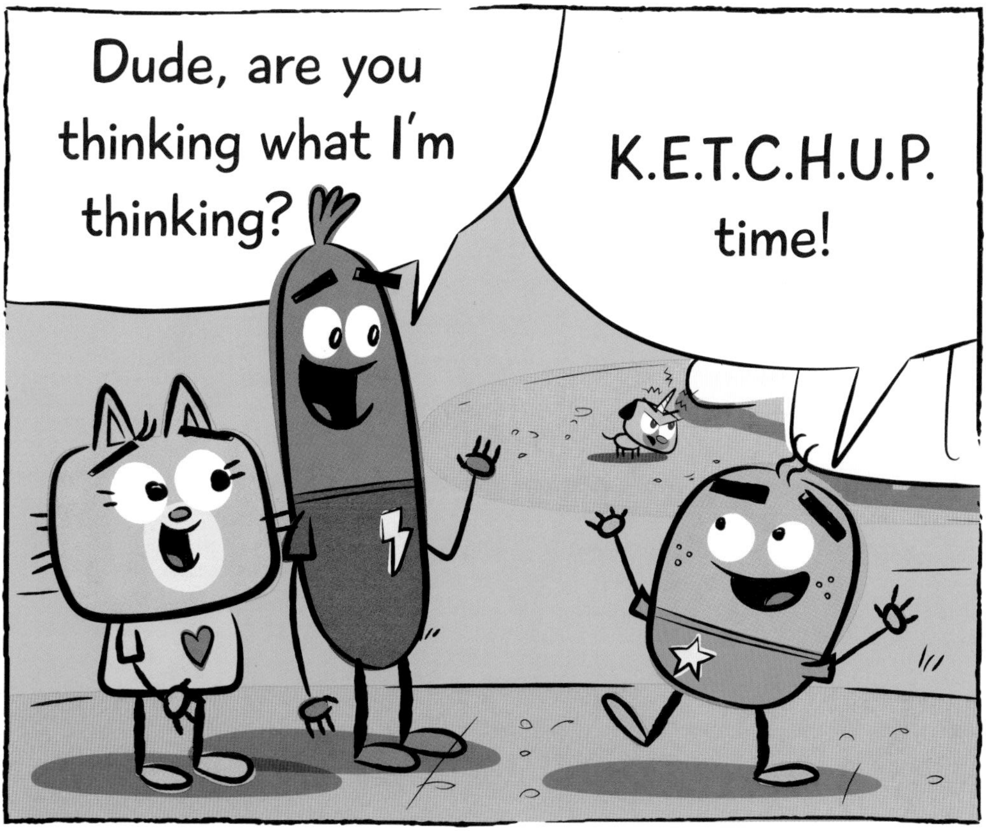
Dude, are you thinking what I'm thinking?
K.E.T.C.H.U.P. time!

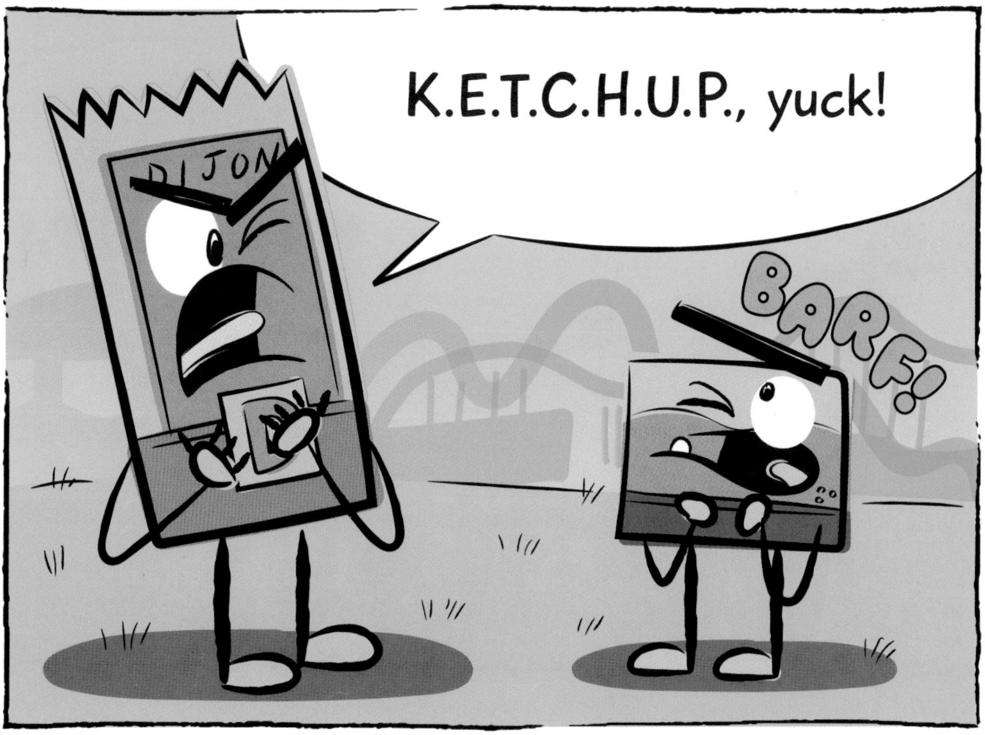
K.E.T.C.H.U.P., yuck!
DIJON
D
BARF!

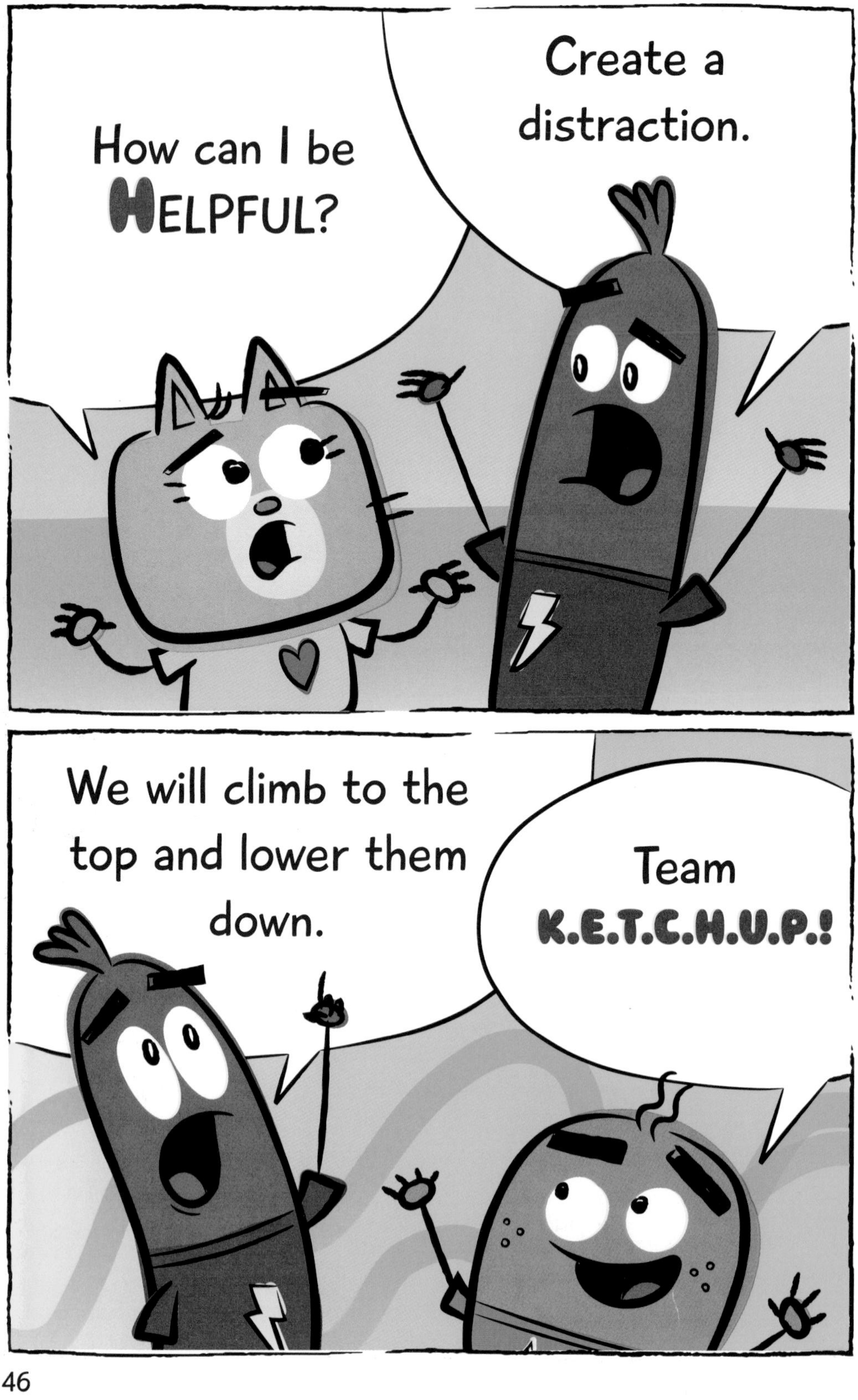
How can I be HELPFUL?
Create a distraction.
We will climb to the top and lower them down.
Team K.E.T.C.H.U.P.!

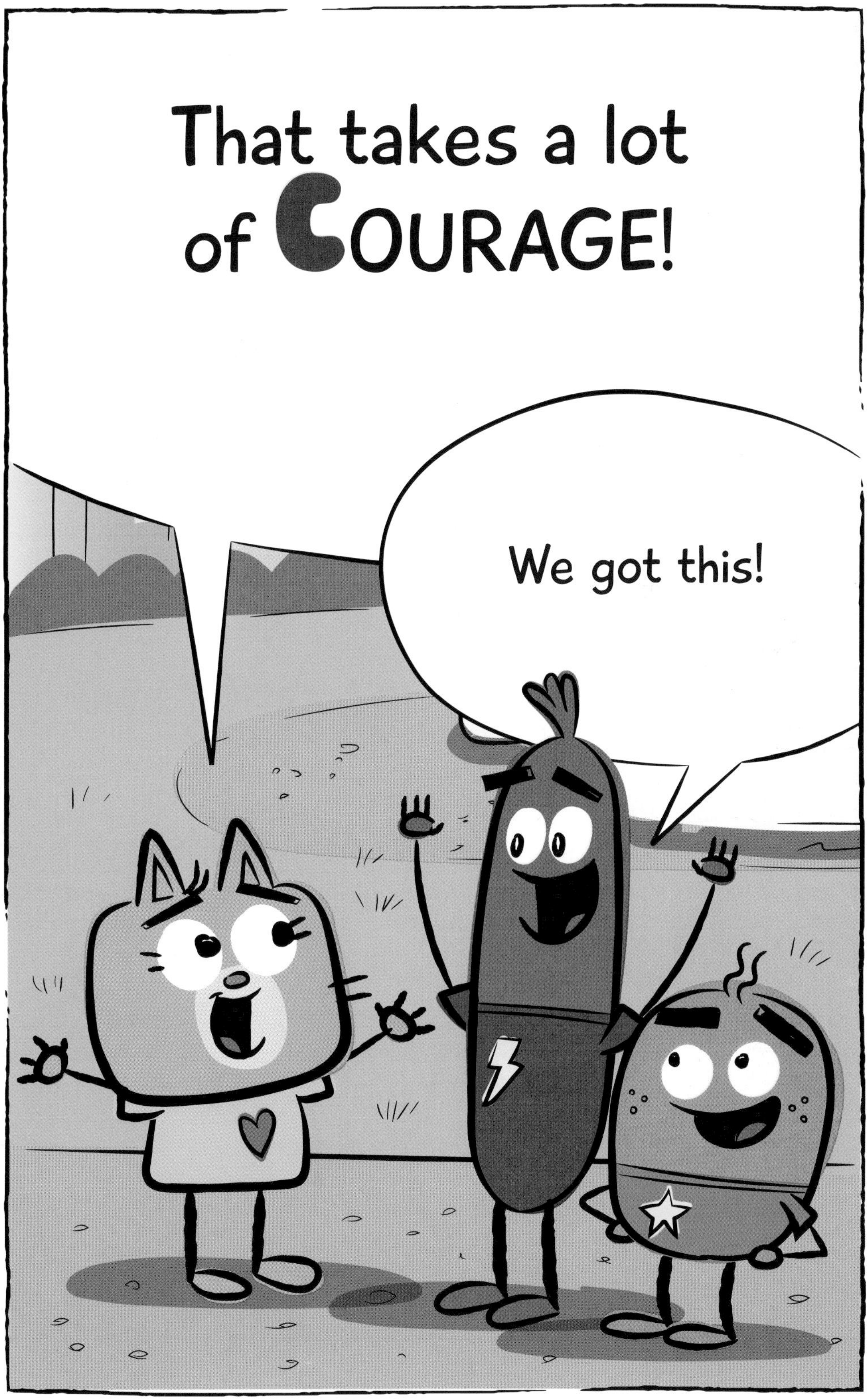
That takes a lot of COURAGE!
We got this!

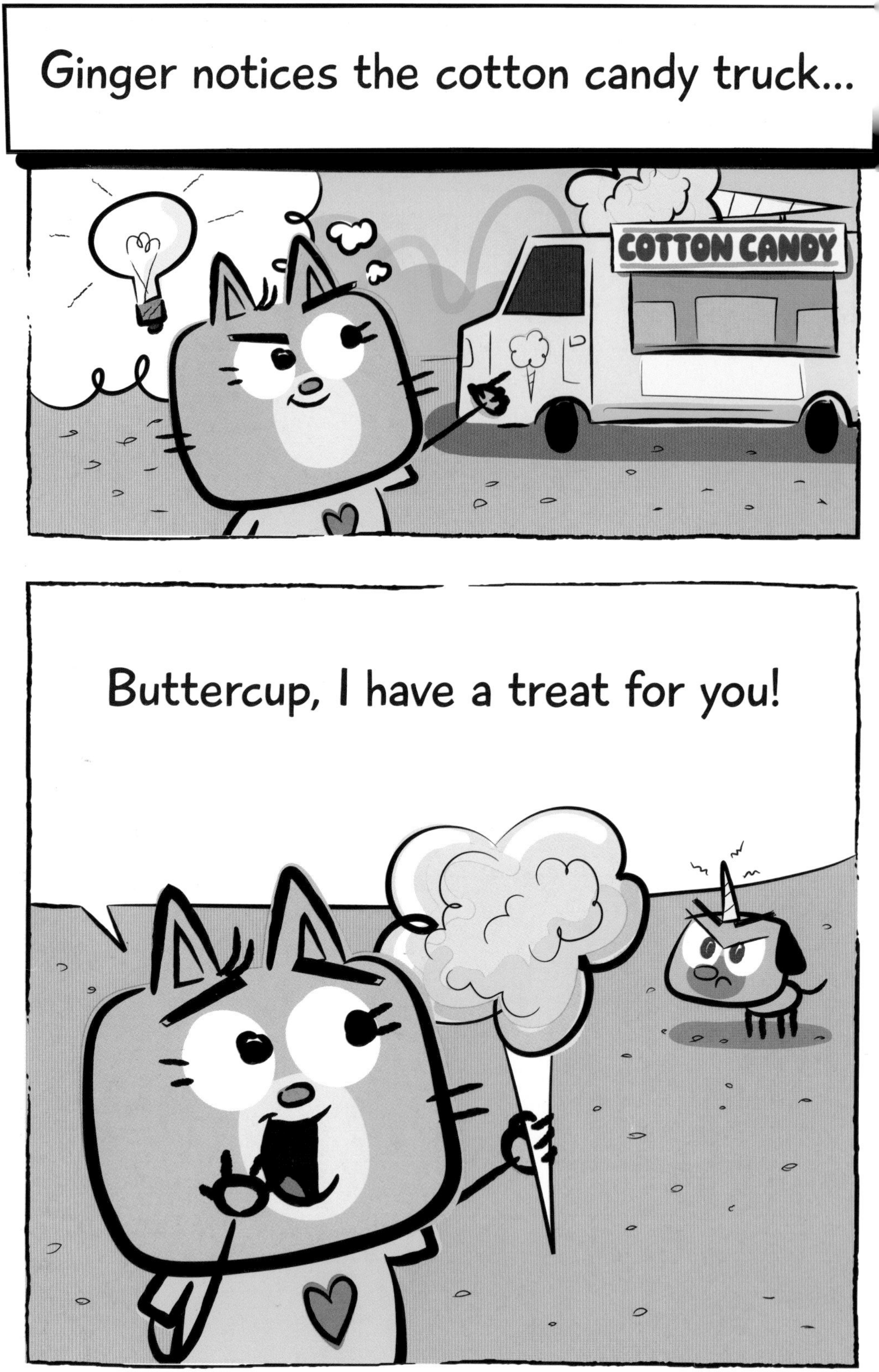
Ginger notices the cotton candy truck...
COTTON CANDY
Buttercup, I have a treat for you!

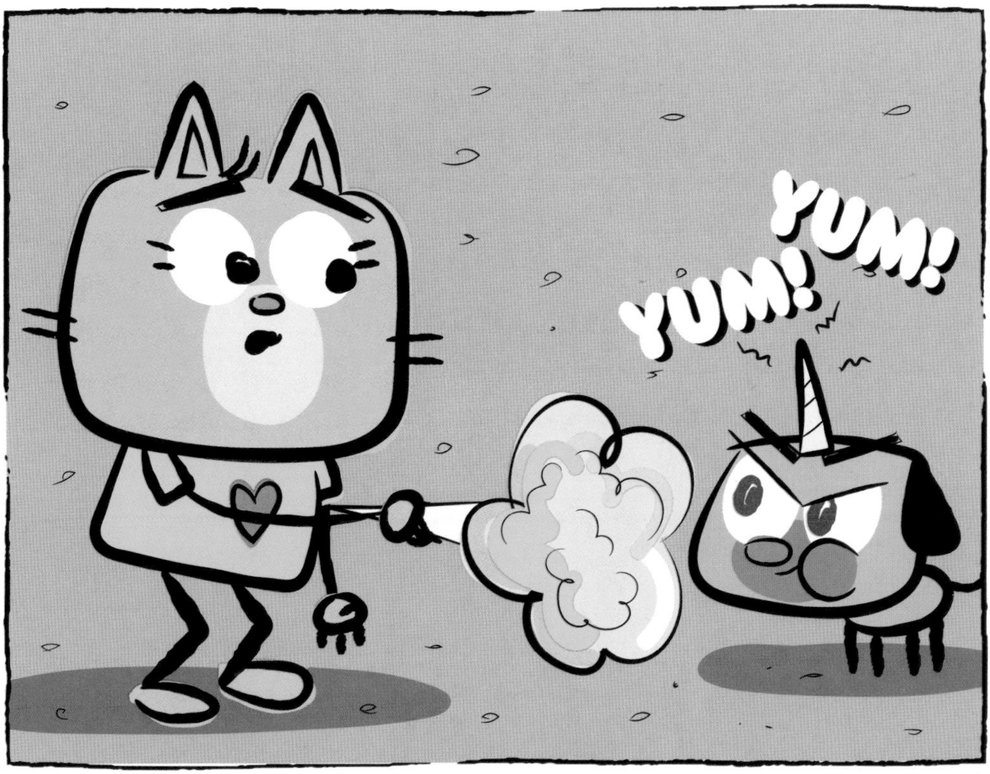
YUM! YUM!

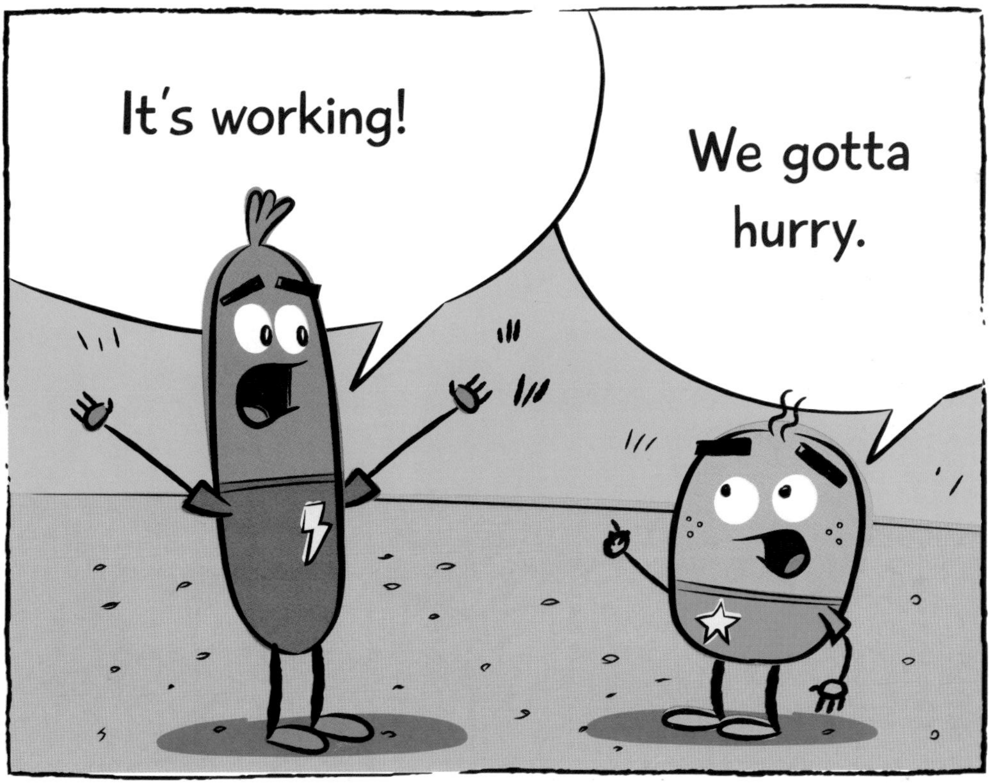
It's working!
We gotta hurry.

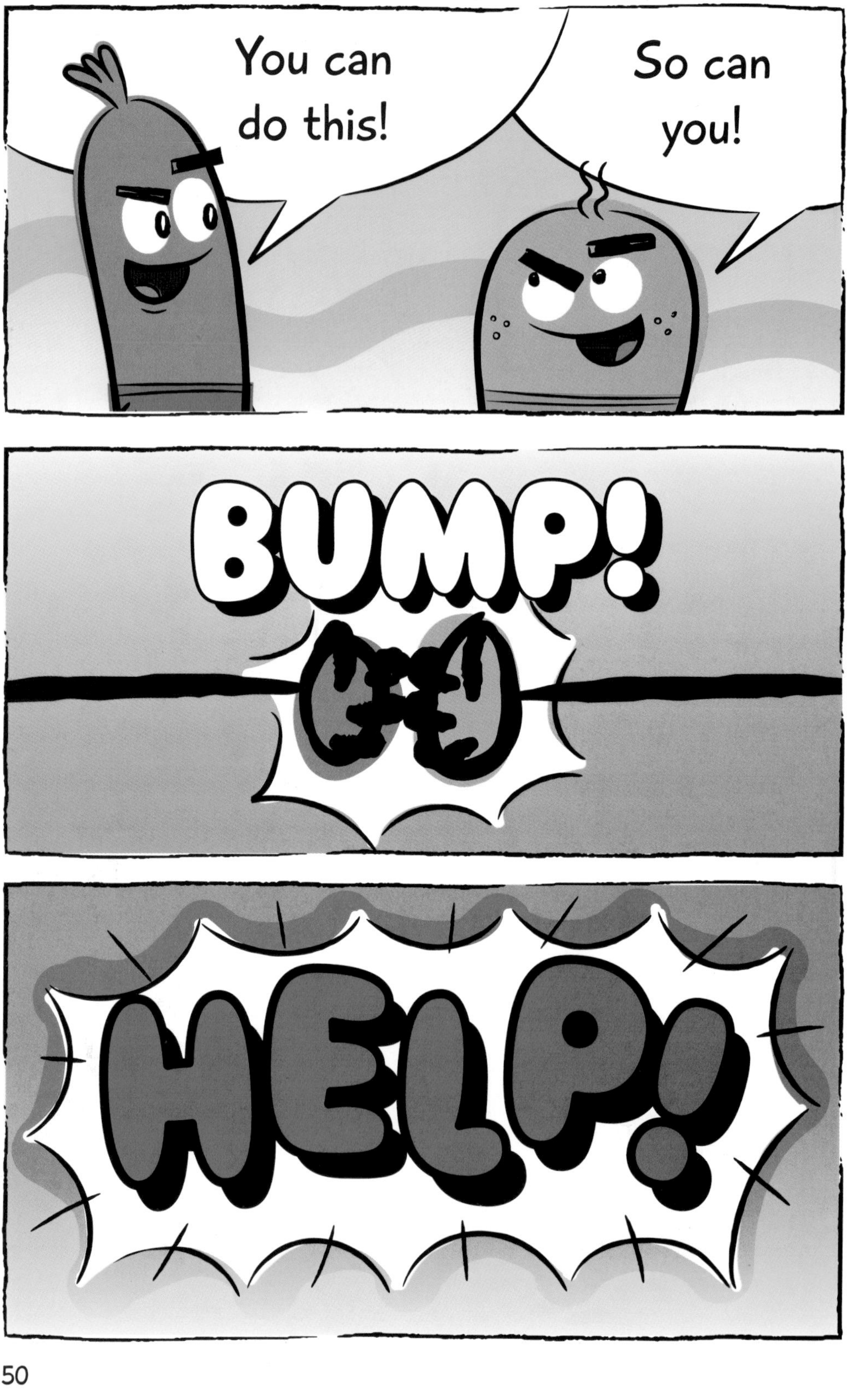
You can do this!
So can you!
BUMP!
HELP!

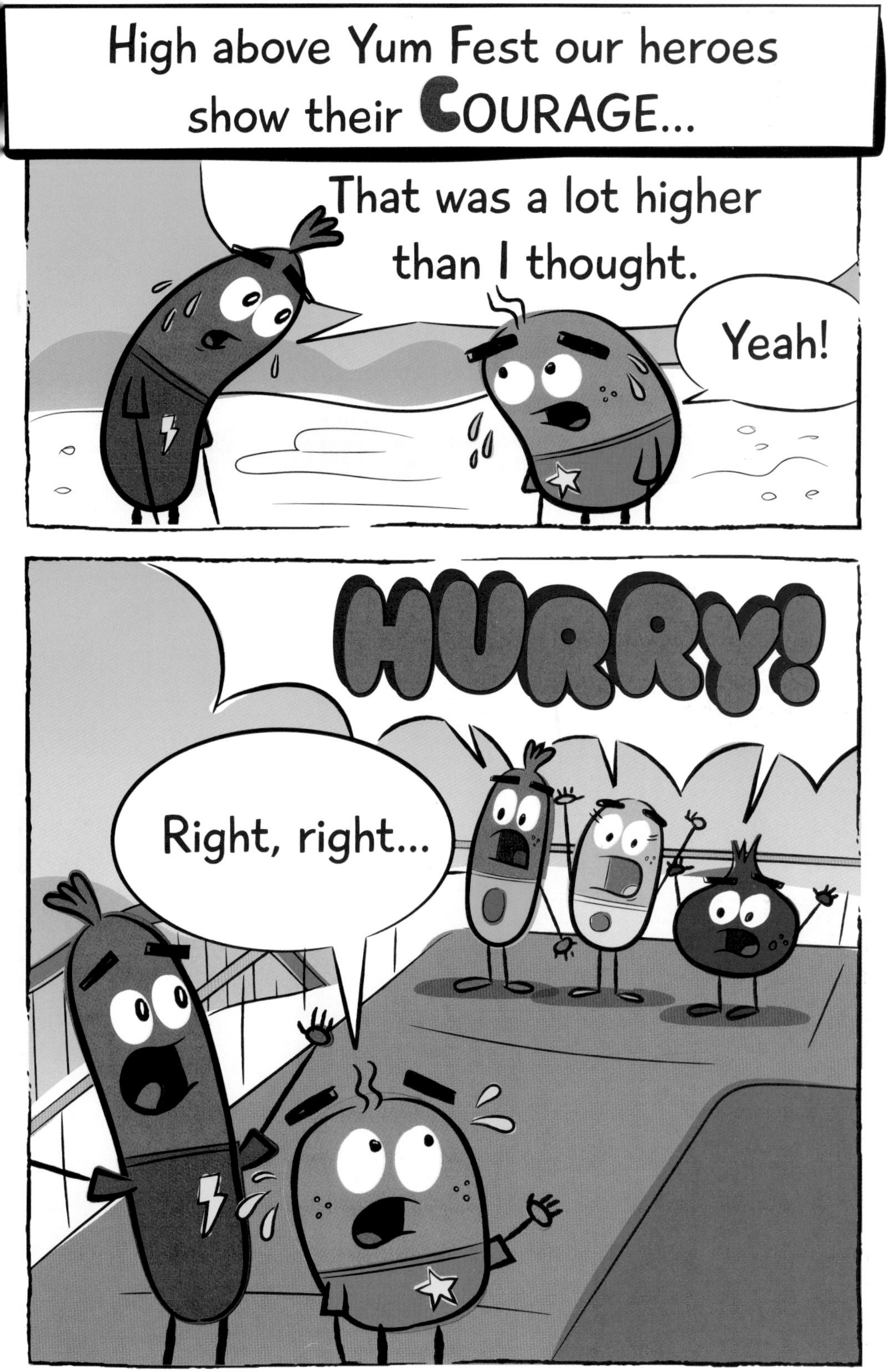
High above Yum Fest our heroes show their COURAGE...
That was a lot higher than I thought.
Yeah!
HURRY!
Right, right...

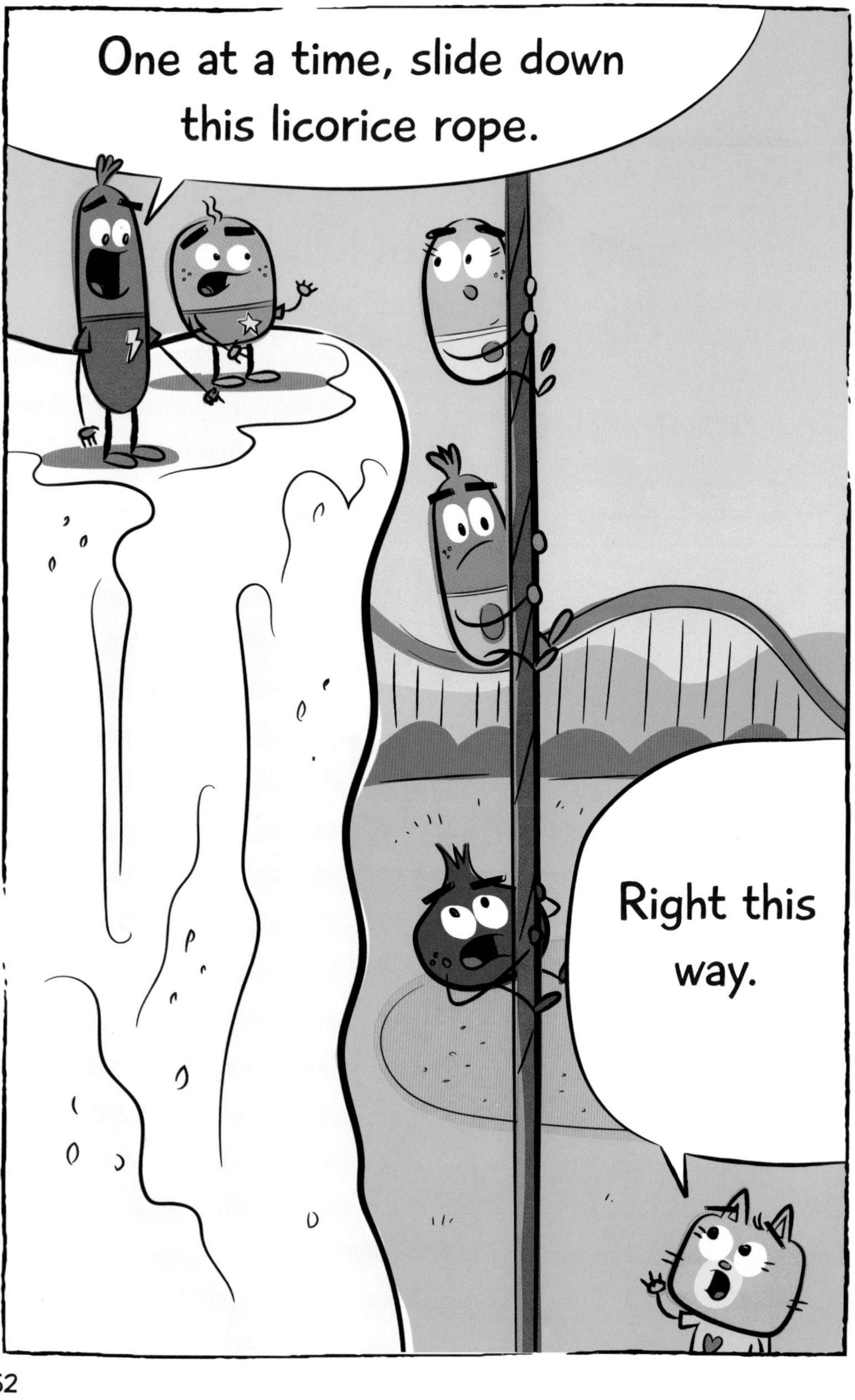
One at a time, slide down this licorice rope.
Right this way.

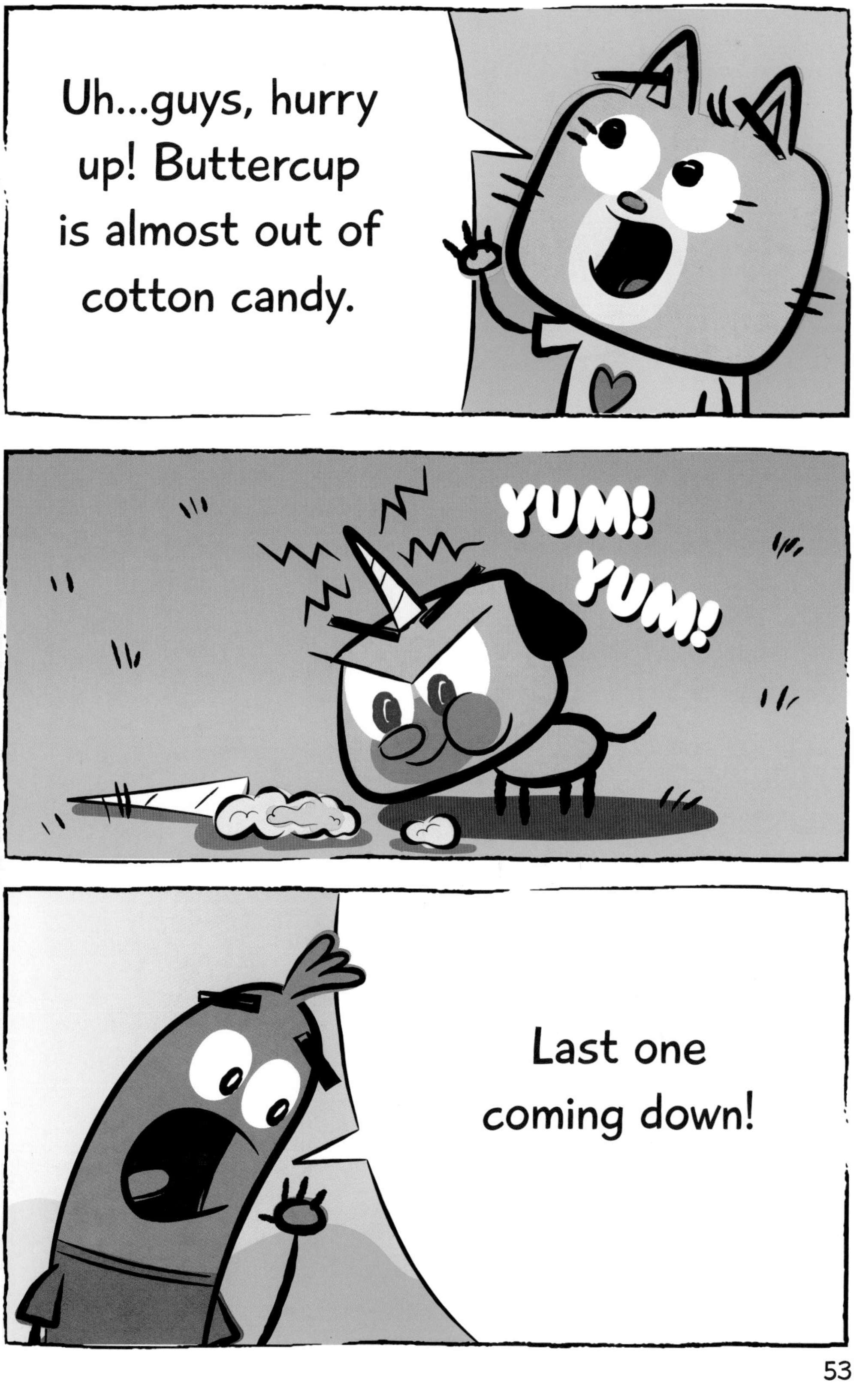
Uh...guys, hurry up! Buttercup is almost out of cotton candy.
YUM! YUM!
Last one coming down!

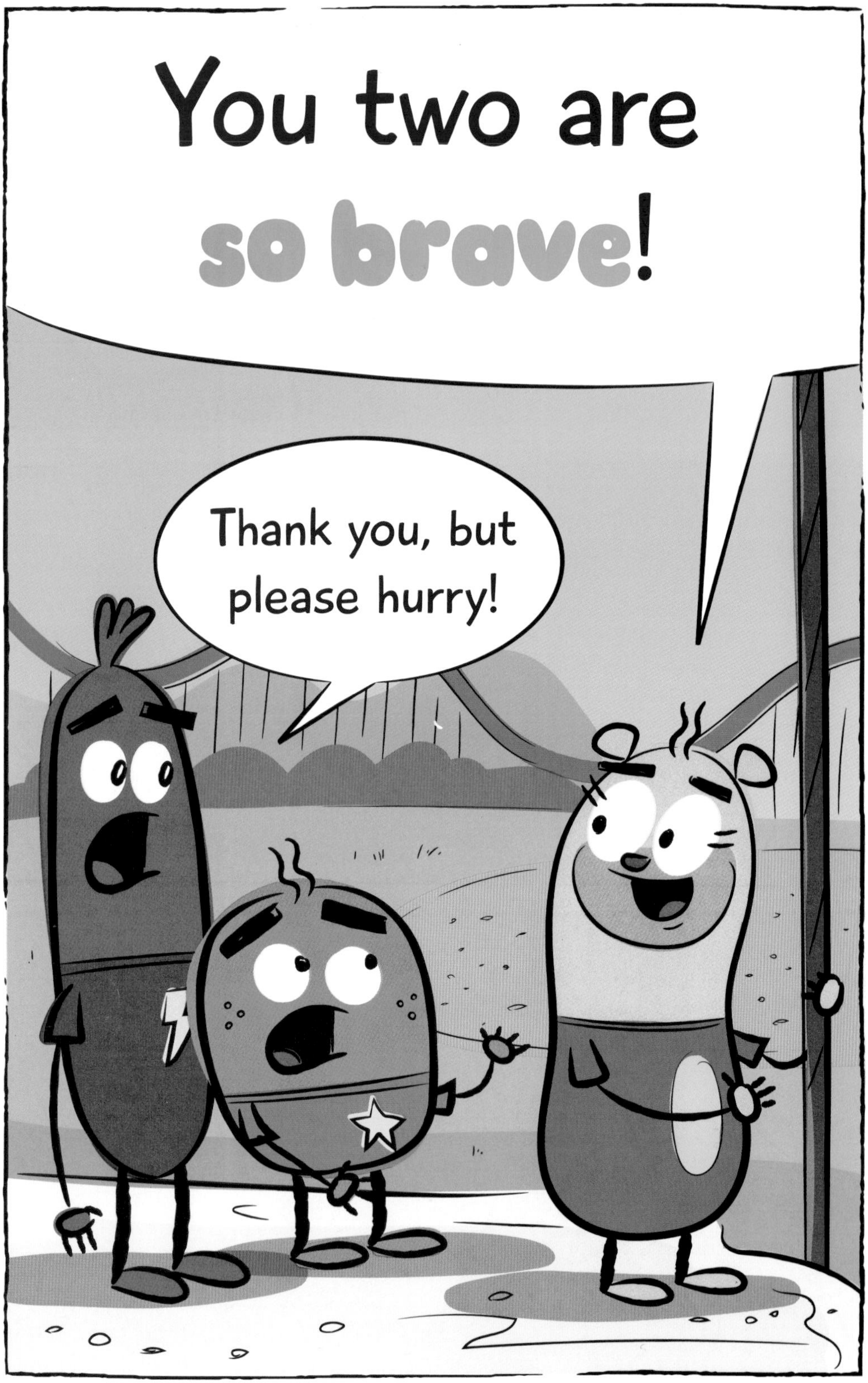
You two are so brave!
Thank you, but please hurry!

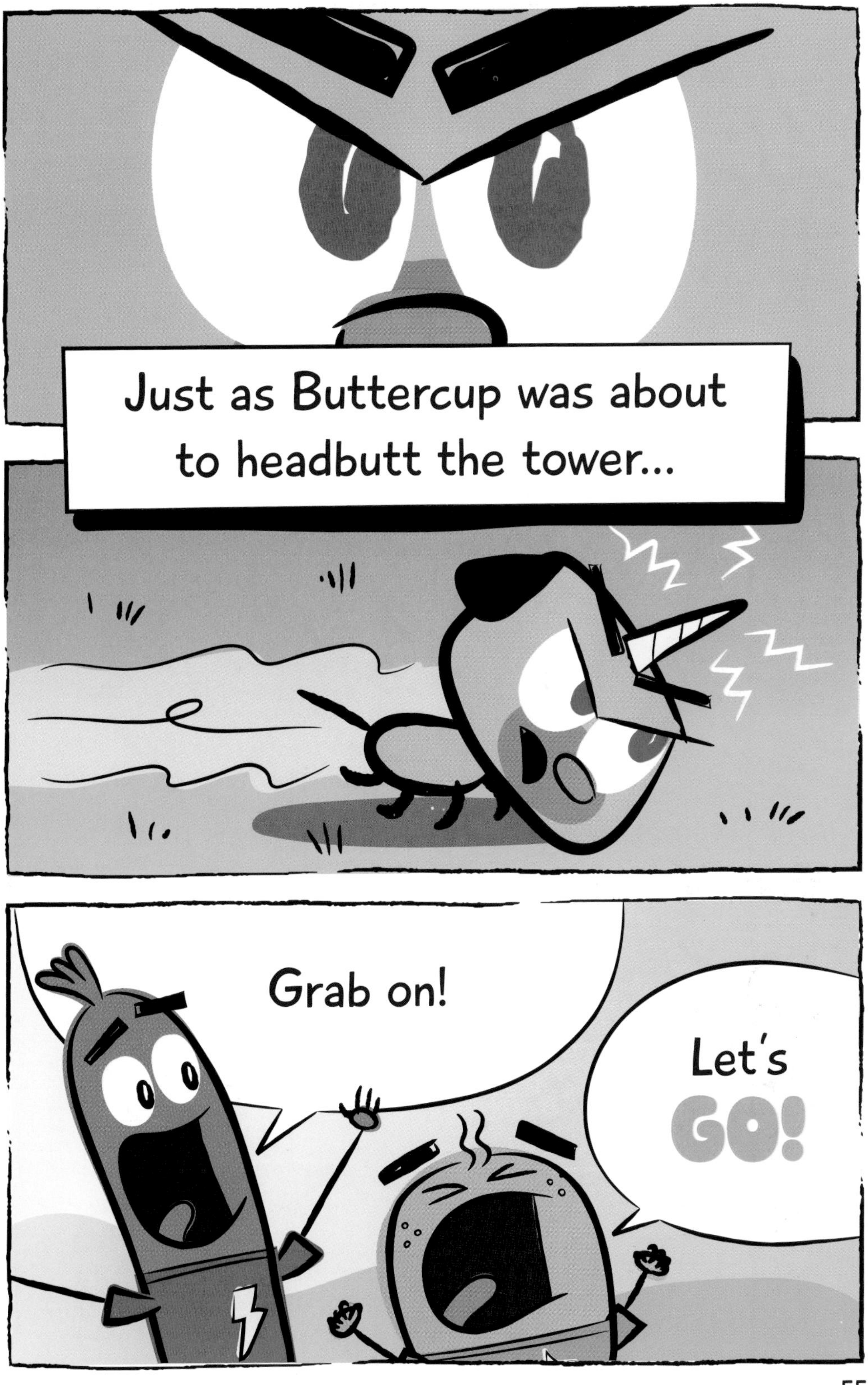
Just as Buttercup was about to headbutt the tower...
Grab on!
Let's GO!

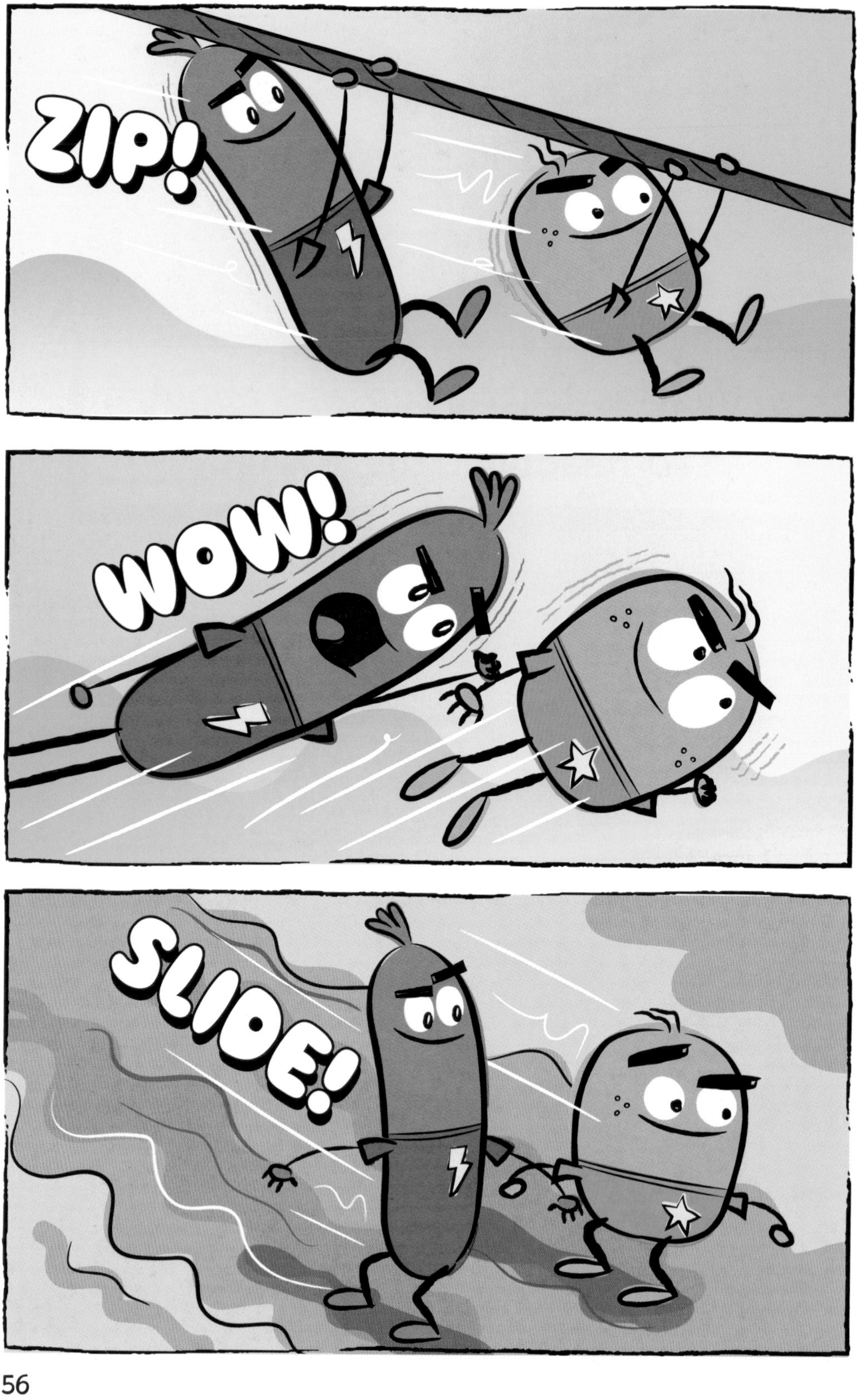
ZIP!
WOW!
SLIDE!

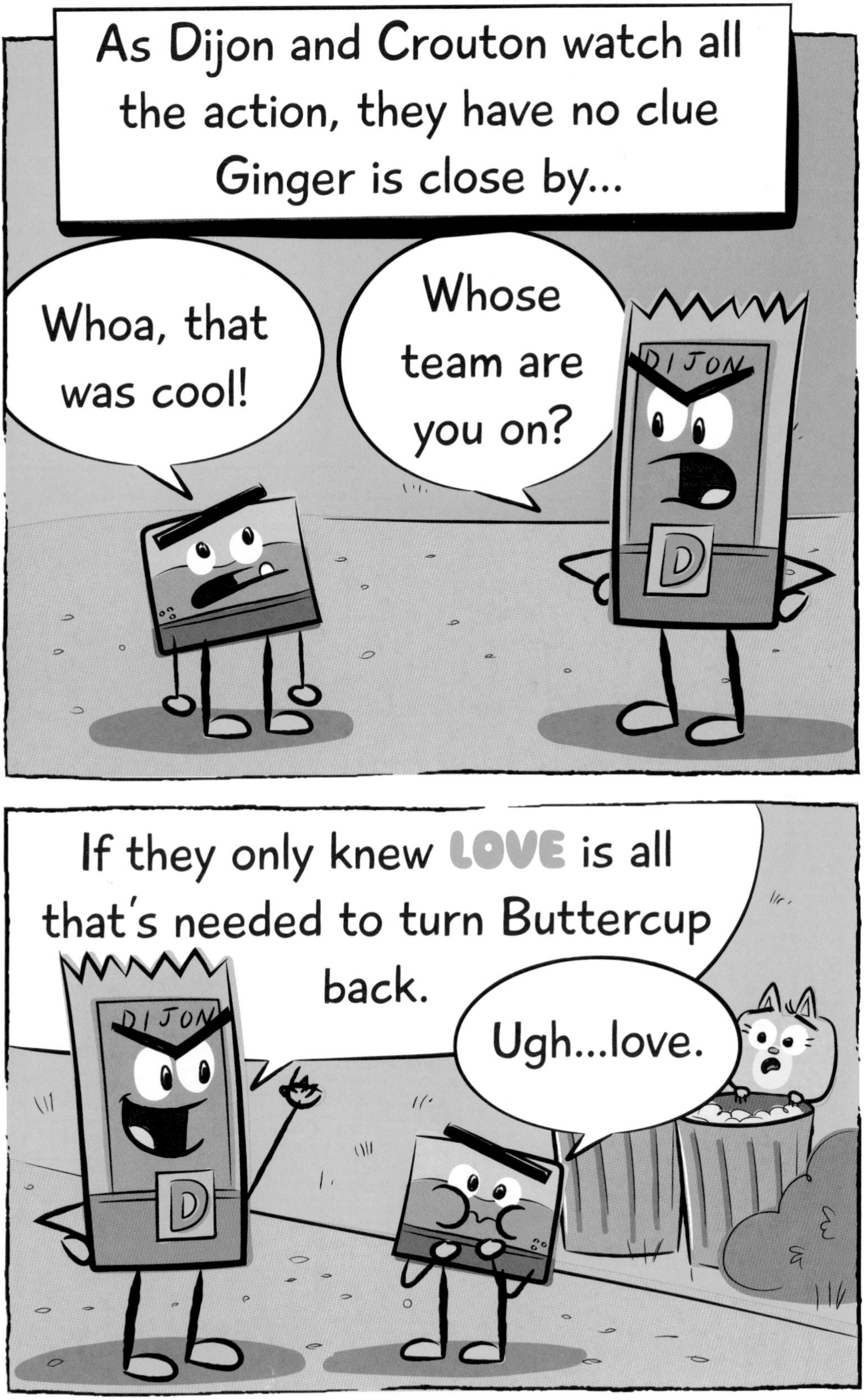
As Dijon and Crouton watch all the action, they have no clue Ginger is close by...
Whoa, that was cool!
Whose team are you on?
DIJON
D
If they only knew LOVE is all that's needed to turn Buttercup back.
DIJON
D
Ugh...love.

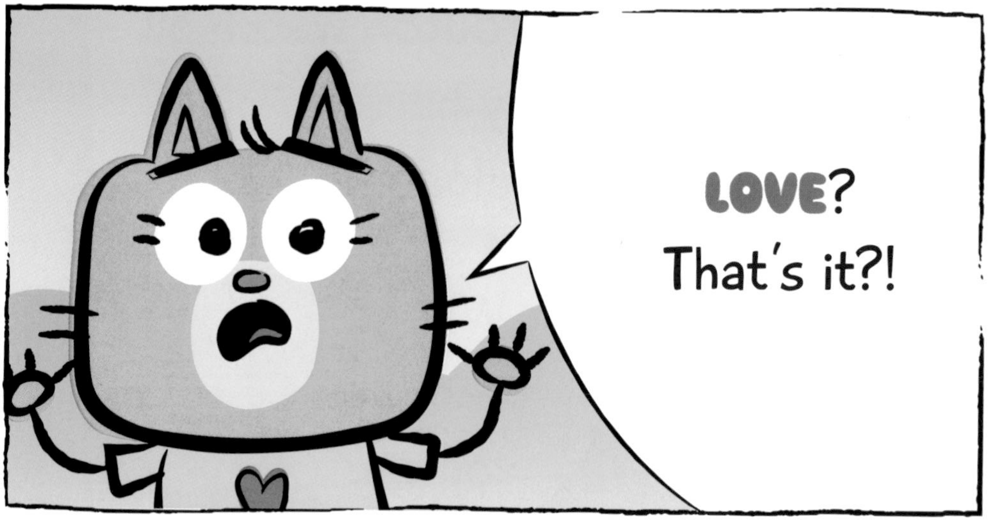
LOVE? That's it?!

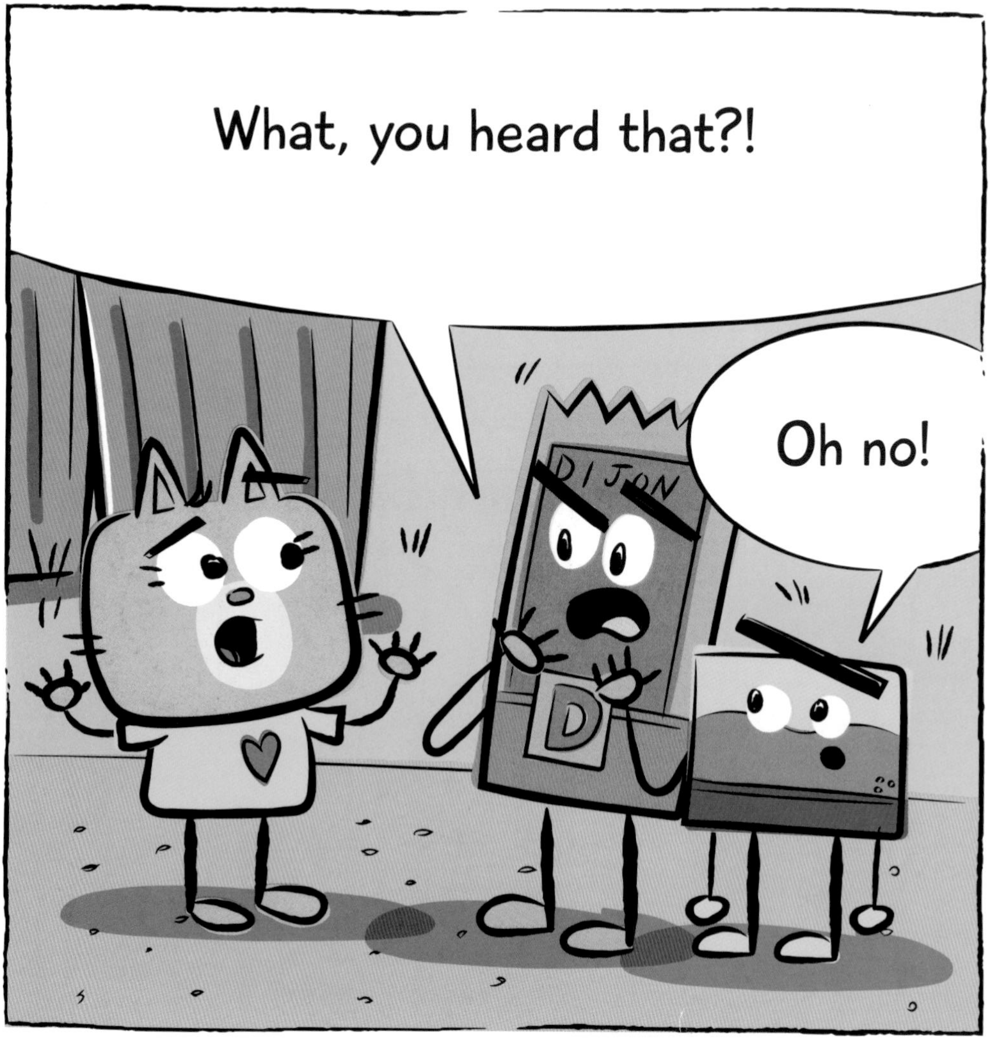
What, you heard that?!
DIJON
D
Oh no!

Chapter 9
LOVE WINS

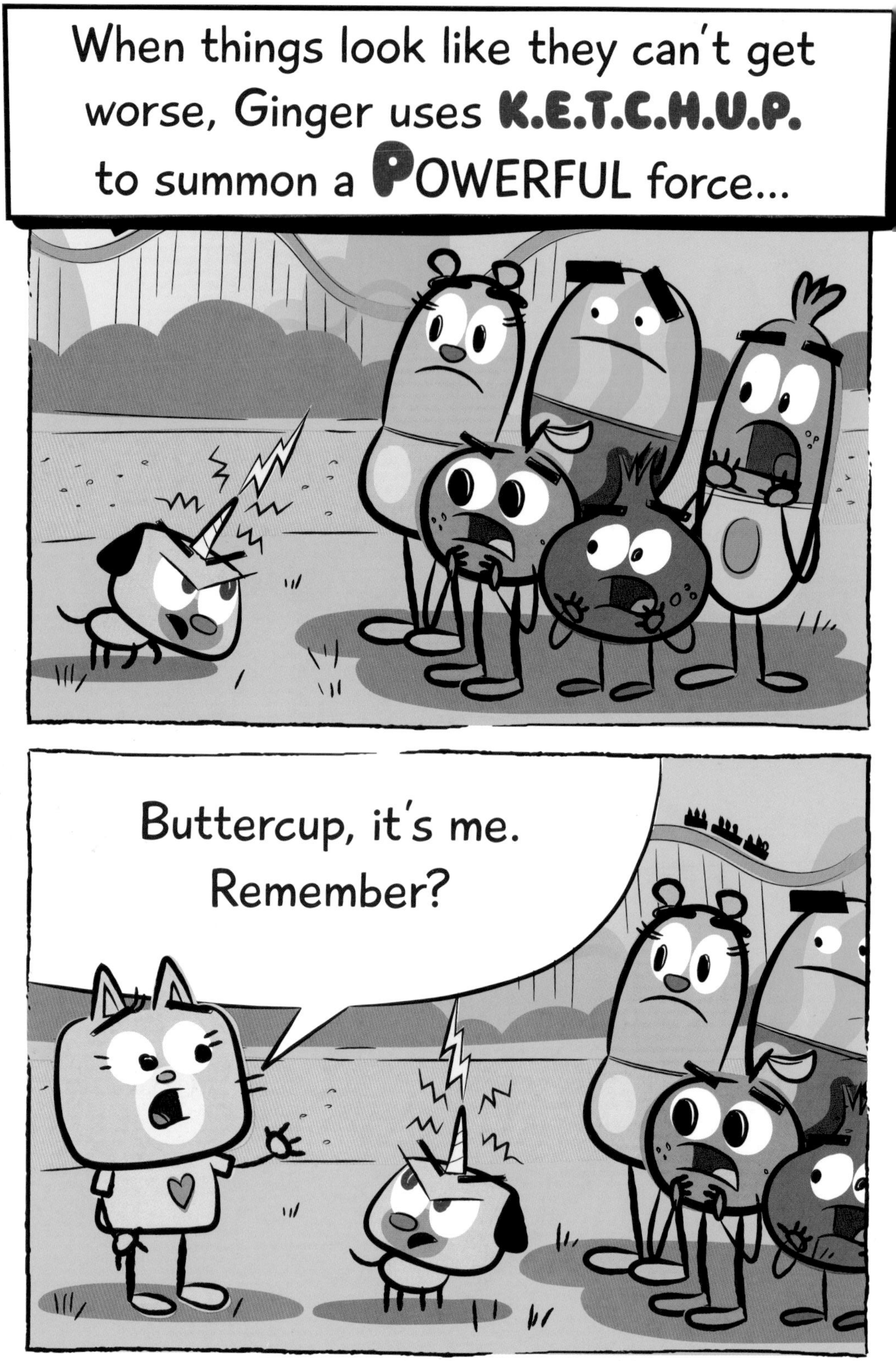
When things look like they can't get worse, Ginger uses K.E.T.C.H.U.P. to summon a POWERFUL force...
Buttercup, it's me. Remember?

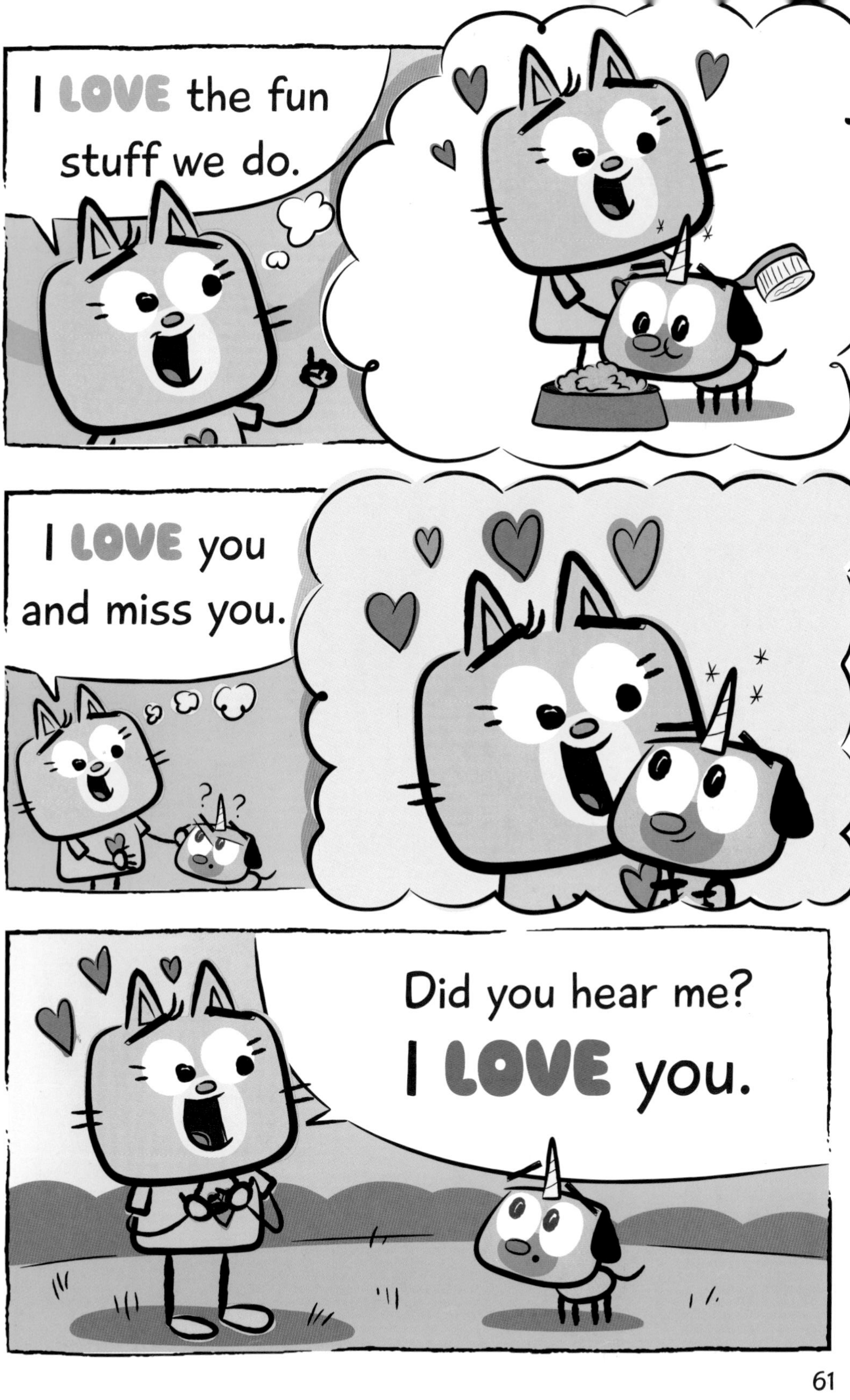
I LOVE the fun stuff we do.
I LOVE you and miss you.
Did you hear me? I LOVE you.

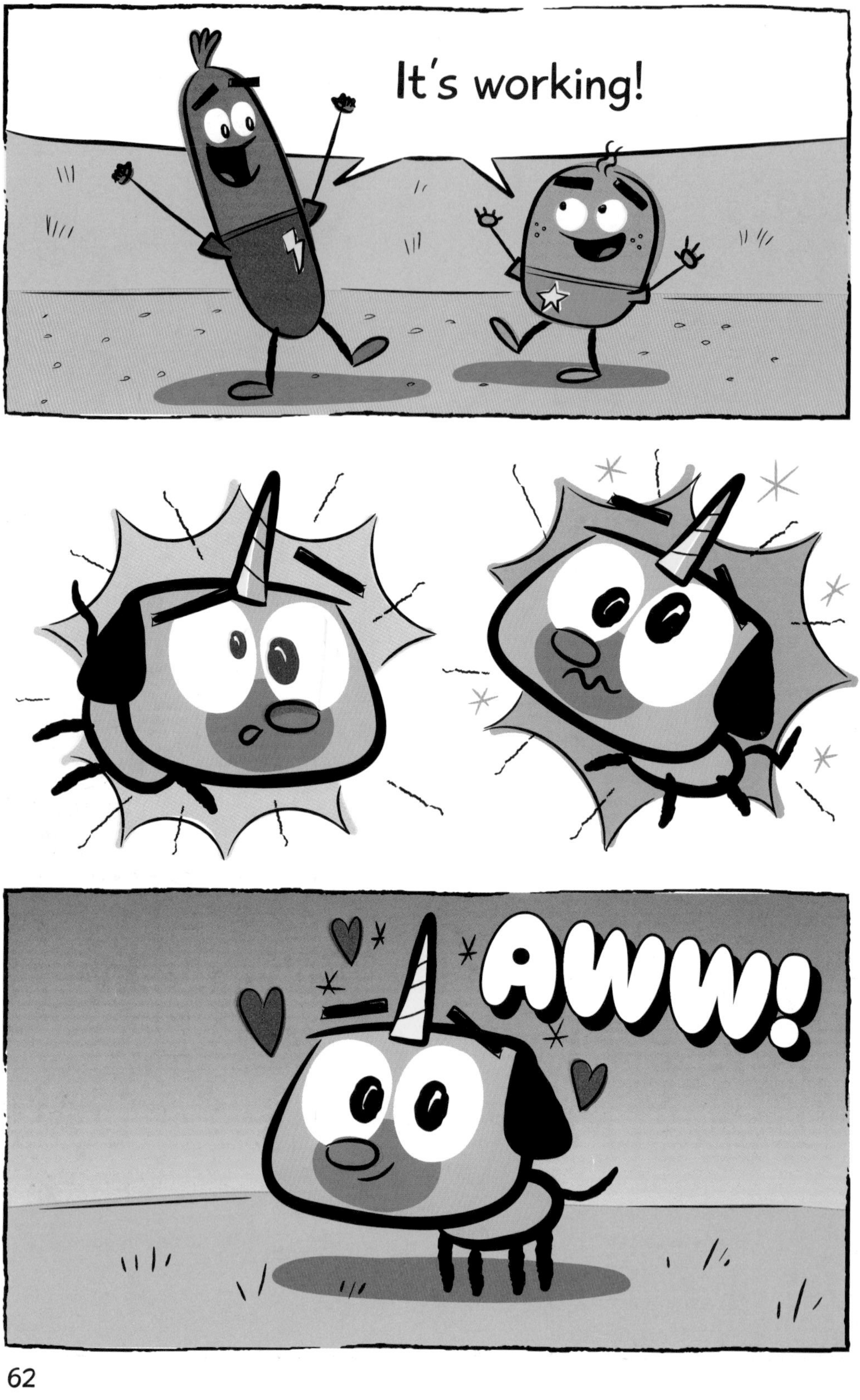
It's working!
AWW!

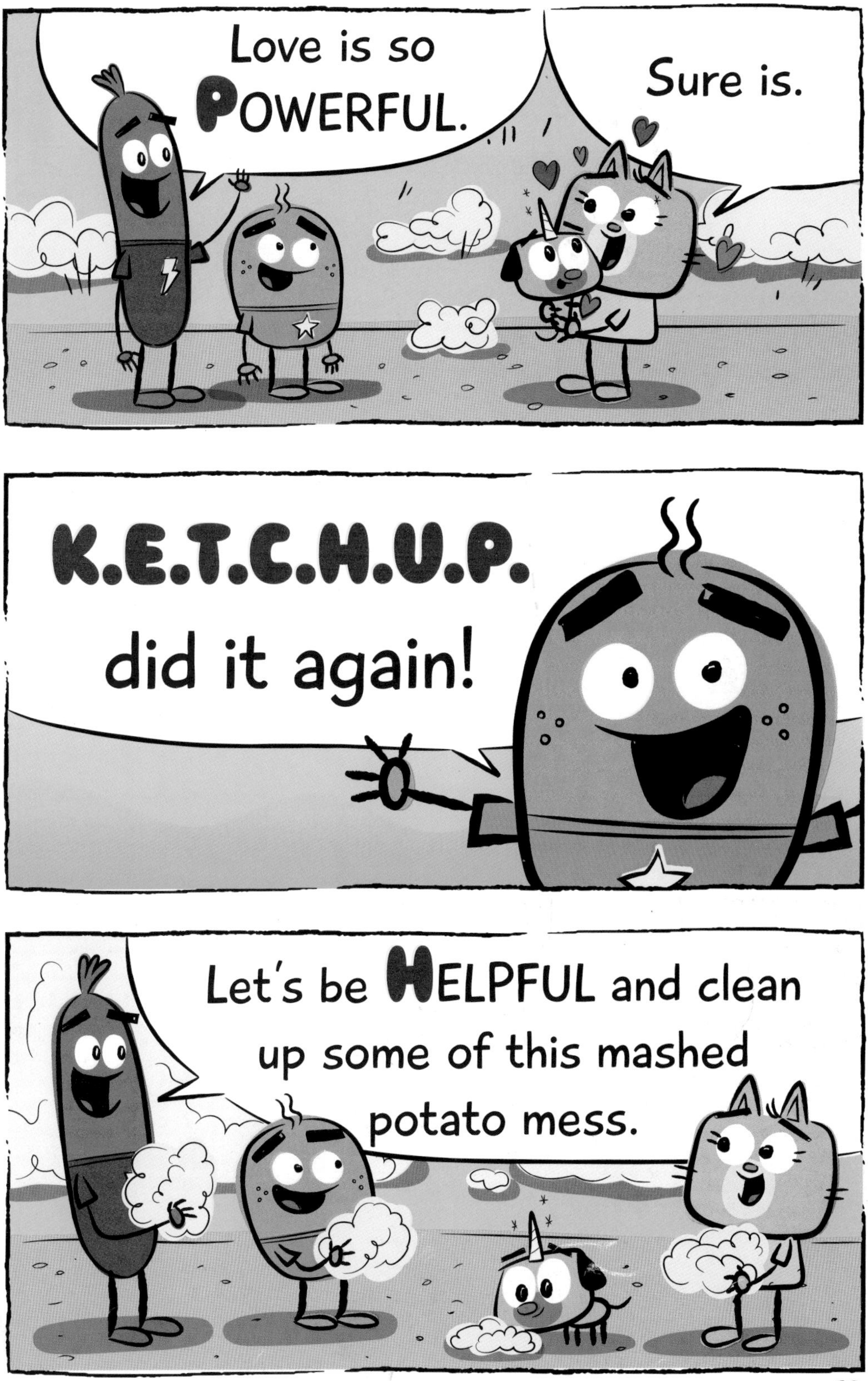
Love is so POWERFUL.
Sure is.
K.E.T.C.H.U.P. did it again!
Let's be HELPFUL and clean up some of this mashed potato mess.

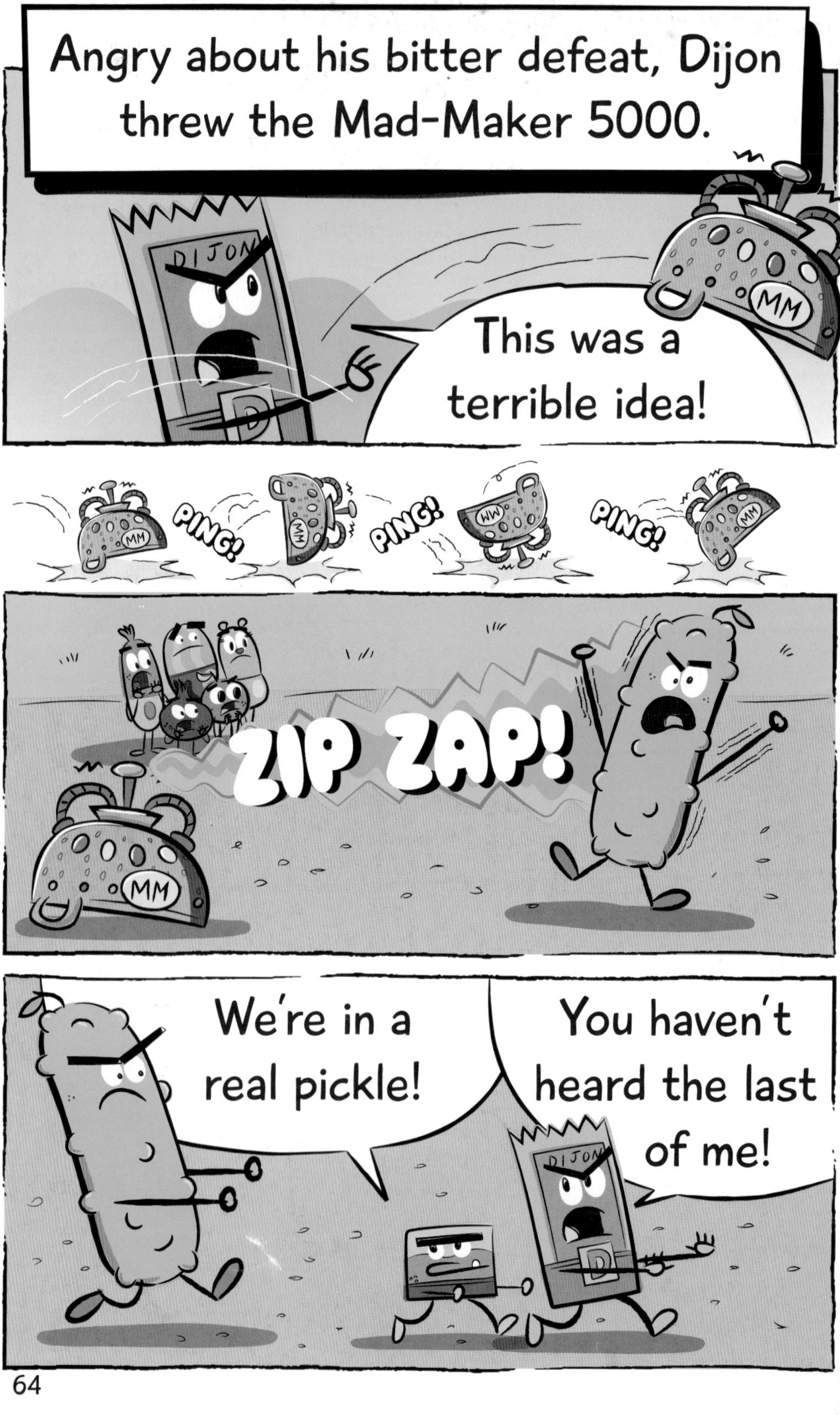
Angry about his bitter defeat, Dijon threw the Mad-Maker 5000.
This was a terrible idea!
PING!
PING!
PING!
ZIP ZAP!
We're in a real pickle!
You haven't heard the last of me!